THE WALLBERG MURDERS

Arlene Romaniuk

American Literary Press, Inc.
Five Star Special Edition
Baltimore, Maryland

The Wallberg Murders

Library of Congress
Cataloging in Publication Data
ISBN 1-56167-739-6

Library of Congress Card Catalog Number:
2002091274

Published by

American Literary Press, Inc.
Five Star Special Edition
8019 Belair Road, Suite 10
Baltimore, Maryland 21236

Manufactured in the United States of America

This book is dedicated to my family.

Thank you for the love and the support you have given me.
You believed in me when I needed it most.

chapter 1

The wind blew gently through the trees as I walked through the park. The lights softly glowing as though a mist covered the shades. I was in another world, and my thoughts were everywhere. Bouncing back and forth from how my day started until it finally came to an end. I could hear laughter through the brush; there were silhouettes of a group of kids going over their evening of fun. I was tired and wanted to get home. A nice warm bath and a glass of wine would finish off my day nicely. It had been a long time since I could go home after my day at the office and relax. I thought back to the day I first came to Daywater and how I was worried that I would be bored because nothing ever happened in this small town. I walked towards my house and could see someone swinging on the porch. As I got closer, I could see it was my partner Dan Gunn. He stood about six foot six with dark shoulder length hair. He always had a big smile on his face and a cup of coffee in his hand. Dan was a good partner and a good man. He had 15 years with the Sheriff's office and had the drive left for another 15 years.

Not much happened in a town as small as Daywater. Most people with a job and a pension stayed in their jobs forever. I decided to move here, trying to escape the rat race of a large city. I had worked on the police force for 10 years in New York City and found that there had to be something better out there, and I was going to find it. A position came up for an Officer's position and I applied. I was surprised when I received a phone call just 5 days later asking me to come on down to Daywater, Illinois for an interview. The voice on the other end said, "You'd better bring your things with you, because we haven't had any other applications." That's when I wondered if I was doing the right thing, by picking up and moving to such a small town.

I arrived 2 days later and was hired by one of the hardest looking men I had ever seen. He stood about five foot ten and weighed about 225 pounds. You could see by the lines on his face that he had been in the business for quite some time and it couldn't have been here. He had a firm handshake and asked me to be seated. His office was out of some old movie. The old creaking wooden floor, the old solid wood desk and the squeaking metal chair. He sat behind his desk and leaned back in his chair. For a moment I thought he would flip right over, but he obviously had the years behind him in that chair, and managed to stay balanced without hesitation. Later I had heard that he, too, came from New York in hopes of escaping the mayhem. He had put in a full term of 25 years with the NYPD and retired. After being at home for a year he found that his heart and soul was left at the Department and felt he needed to get back into the circle. However, he felt that it would be nice at this point for him to go to a smaller community to continue with his career. He had seen enough tragedy while in the NYPD and decided to apply for a position with the County Sheriff's office. As he was a well respected detective, the opportunity of becoming sheriff came right to his doorstep. After consultation with his wife they moved to Daywater.

Well, he began by advising me that I was to call him Max; it was a name he used throughout his whole career. He didn't want to be called "sheriff" or "sir." He believed in a casual approach to policing and that had to start at the office.

"So, what brings you to the metropolis of Daywater?"

"I like the path my career has taken, but I am tired of the long hours and the continual mayhem in New York. I want to stay in law enforcement, but I need to know that there is still some good out there."

"Well, you have come to the right place" said Max with a grin on his face. "You won't find too much action here, but you may find it a little boring at first. You'll work into it slowly, and if you don't, well you know you can always go back to New York"

I just smiled and said, "Well, what exactly will I be doing on a routine basis?"

"Oh this and that, basically town patrols, filing complaints, investigating accidents and upon occasion asking speeders to slow down."

I caught the advising speeders to slow down and wondered if in fact they have ever given out a speeding ticket. I wouldn't concern myself with those little details for now. I was just curious to find out where I was going to settle in this office. I looked over and spotted two desks facing each other and assumed one would be mine, so I cleared my throat and said, "So which one of these desks is mine?"

He looked over and said, "Oh, it's the one facing north."

I walked over and placed my handbag on the desk. The chair looked like it has been there since the building was built, but when I sat down I found it to be quite comfortable. The desk seemed barren. There wasn't a piece of paper or a file anywhere. I thought to myself again, did I do the right thing?

Just then my future partner walked in and Max stood up and said "Gunn, I'd like you to meet your new partner, Meghan King."

"Hi, you can call me Meg"

"Great, and you can call me Gunn, everyone does."

"So now that we have all met each other, Gunn could you take Meg and show her the town, introduce her to some of the store owners and let her get a chance to know everyone? This is a tight knit community, and the only way to survive is to get to know who's who." Gunn stepped in front of me and reached over to hold the door open. Just before we got outside Max yelled, "and after he has shown you around, take the rest of the day off to get settled."

Gunn nodded and then turned to me and said, "It'll be hard for you to get used to the peacefulness of the country living, but you are going to find you will love it."

"Yes, but what exactly do you people do on your days off?"

"Not much, maybe do a little fishing, that's about it."

As we walked down the main street, you could see people raising their hands and waving to Gunn. "I better take you to meet Bill. He owns the grocery store here in town, and the gas station, runs the post office and does just about everything else there is to do here."

"He must have been here for a few years then?"

"Yes, he was one of the founders of Daywater. Bill, I'd like you to meet my new partner, Meg."

This withered hand reached out to shake mine. I leaned forward, and he held on to my hand and gave it a brisk shake, "Welcome aboard Meg, it's nice to see someone as pretty as you come and live in our fine town."

I'm sure I turned every shade of red, but I went on to say, "Well, thank you, Bill, I hope I can be of service to you, and if you need anything, just let me know."

He smiled like my grandfather would have if he had been standing in front of me right then. So I smiled back and Gunn said, "Well, we have to be moving along, there is a lot of ground to cover." I couldn't imagine what he meant by "a lot of ground to cover." There were only 100 people in the entire town, but I followed along side of him, enjoying the fresh spring air and the warm sun filtering through the clouds.

"So what brings you to Daywater?"

"I needed a change"

"Oh, like Max and I? It can get to be a bit much in the big city, eh?"

"Yes, I knew it was time to leave when I'd wake up after about four hours of sleep and hear nothing but sirens racing back and forth, and I'd lay there wondering who died now, should I go down to the precinct, they probably need me."

"We have both been there so no explanation is necessary."

"I am worried though Gunn."

"About what?"

"Well, how long does it take to settle into a place like this? I mean, I know it is a close knit community and in most cases it is hard to get inside the niche."

"You won't have any trouble. You are the first female to walk into this town from the outside, never mind that you are an officer of the law."

"Yes, and that is what I am afraid of."

Just then a well-dressed lady approached us and said, "Oh my, Gunn, and who is this sweet innocent child you have with you today?" Her tone was that of a sarcastic nature crossed between curious.

"Sabella, I'd like you to meet Meg. She is our new officer and will be of any assistance you might require,"

"Well, Gunn, you have done just fine on your own, and I don't think there is anything that Meg can do that you haven't already done."

She was very protective of Gunn. I found myself jumping in at that moment and saying, "I'm sure Gunn has been outstanding in performing all of his duties. I hope to learn something from him."

I think for a moment I may have actually had her attention, but then quickly lost it when she very gracefully said, "Gunn, Jack and I would like to have you over for dinner tonight. Six o'clock, and if you like, you can bring her."

I wasn't very pleased to be referred to as "her," however, it was a good opportunity for me to break into the circle. Gunn confirmed that we would both be there, without even asking me if I was available. I guess he knew there wasn't much else to do in Daywater. As we proceeded down the street he said, " It would be good to get on the good side of the Wallbergs, they are very powerful people in this town; you might say they have the money that paves the streets."

So I nodded and said, "That will be fine with me, so will you be coming to pick me up seeing as I have no idea where they live?"

"You mean you didn't see the white cathedral when you entered town?"

"No , actually I was surprised at the size of the town and was busy looking down the barren street that was directly in front of me."

"Well, you will have the grand tour, I can assure you, and it won't be by Sabella. Jack will take you around. Sabella tends to be a bit beyond us average people, or so she thinks. She enjoys flirting with me in front of her husband rather than taking the time to meet, and possibly get to know, someone as fine as yourself. That's just the way she is, but you'll be O.K. Her husband is a wonderful man and is well liked by the townspeople."

"So, what time will you be at my place. I'm over at the boarding house at the end of Elm."

"I'll be there at 5:30 sharp. That will give us enough time to drive you around and show you the river on the other side of town. It's close enough to the Wallbergs so we won't be late."

At that point, Gunn pointed out that there was no need for me to go back to the office, so we said our goodbyes and walked our separate ways. It was hot and humid and I wanted to get in a shower and freshen up before it was time to leave again.

The old boarding house was run by an elderly lady by the name of Ruby, who was as pleasant and kind as they get. Ruby was sitting on the front veranda when I walked up the street. She raised her hand and waved. "So dear, how was your first day?"

"Well, I guess it was O.K., but I haven't done anything."

"Oh, in a few days I'm sure something will come up, and you will be able to feel like you have accomplished something. Why don't you have a seat here on the swing and I'll get you some lemonade."

I nodded for at that moment lemonade sounded wonderful. Ruby disappeared inside the house to retrieve a glass of ice cold lemonade. I sat swinging on the front porch, feeling like the most relaxed individual on this planet. My mind was off thinking about how comfortable I felt here, when Slam! I must have jumped five feet in the air. I looked up and there was a fellow getting out of his car and coming towards me.

"Good day!"

So I responded, "Hello there, beautiful day outside, isn't it?"

"It sure is. I was wondering if you could help me find my way. I seem to have taken a wrong turn somewhere along the way and ended up here in Daywater."

"Certainly, where is it you would like to go? I'm not originally from Daywater but if I can be of help."

"Well, I'm looking for a place called Charlesville. Have you heard of it?"

"No, actually I haven't, but if you want to wait a moment, Ruby will be right out, and I'm sure she can help you with directions."

As we waited for Ruby to come outside again, he removed his hat from his head and started to fan himself. I watched him closely and tended to size him up carefully. After all, those years of police training haven't been for anything. He appeared as though he had driven a long time. His eyes looked weary and his clothes wrinkled. He looked like he could use a shower and a change of clothing. Just then Ruby came through the screen door, "Hello and welcome, are you looking for a place to stay today?"

"No, actually I'm looking for Charlesville. I think I probably made a wrong turn somewhere along the way."

"Oh, do you have family there?"

"Well, uh, no, just going for a day or so."

"What would you possibly have to do in Charlesville for a day?"

At that moment, I could see this fellow getting agitated over the questions he was being asked. His face was turning a slight shade of pink, and the perspiration seemed to be running down his forehead over his face and down his chest. Then again Ruby started up with saying, "Well, you know if you are looking for work there, you may as well turn around and go right back from where you came. You would have a better chance of finding work here then Charlesville. You know, you look so familiar, did you say you were originally from these parts?"

Then rather abruptly the fellow said, "Look, do you know where it is and how I can get there, or should I go elsewhere?"

"Oh, I'm sorry, I didn't realize you were in a rush. All you have to do is go back to the main highway, turn left and drive about 15 miles, you'll see a gas station and two houses. That's Charlesville."

He immediately turned around and without saying thank you, jumped in his late 70s Chevrolet. The car looked like it was on its last legs. There was rust along the entire side of the vehicle. I looked over at Ruby and she had a surprised look on her face.

"He was certainly in a hurry now, wasn't he?"

"Well, I don't know of anyone who would want to go to Charlesville other than to get gas. There is nothing there, not even a place to stay. I imagine he'll be coming back through here on his way home, wherever that might be."

I picked up my glass of lemonade and had a large drink. It tasted as fresh as the morning air. The lemons had been freshly squeezed and just the right amount of sugar was added. It made your mouth water just at the thought of having another drink.

"This is wonderful Ruby. Thank you so much."

"Oh, I believe in fresh lemons and raw sugar. That is the only way to drink lemonade, not this powder you buy in the stores nowadays."

She took the words right out of my mouth. Up until today, I drank the store bought powder, and it was nothing like this. I picked up the glass and finished what little was left. "Well, Ruby, I guess I have been invited to the Wallbergs for dinner this evening, so I better go and freshen up."

"The Wallbergs? Do you know them?"

"No, but Gunn has been invited, and he was asked to bring me."

"Well, you just watch yourself there girl, the Wallbergs can be your best friend or your worst enemy."

I was surprised that sweet little Ruby would make a statement like that, but I thought she has been here as long as they have so I would be cautious not to burn any bridges.

"Thank you, Ruby, for the warning. I'll be careful."

As I walked up the stairs to my bedroom, I could hear the birds singing and the gravel crunching as a car passed by. This was a small town, but I think I was going to like it. I looked at the clock by my bed, and it was a quarter to 5:00. My God, how could the day have gone so quickly. I hurried into the shower, got dressed, and was just about ready when I heard Gunn on the front porch talking to Ruby.

"So, Ruby, how have things been lately? Any new boarders besides Meg?"

"No, but you know, I think I probably will have one later today."

"Oh, and why is that?"

"Well, this fellow, and he sure does look familiar, stopped by looking for directions on how to get to Charlesville. He said he had to go there for a bit. But when I asked him if he knew anyone there, he just quickly changed the subject and got the directions and took off."

"Yeah, I don't know why anyone would want to go to Charlesville, unless they needed gas."

Just then I opened the screen door and said, You know, that is just what Ruby said."

"Well now, don't you look nice."

Gunn made me blush. I wore a bright yellow dress, plain but fitting. I had on a pair of white sandal pumps and had my hair tied up on top of my head. There were a few hairs trailing down around my face and down the back of my neck. On days like today, it was hard to keep cool with my long thick hair. So, up seemed to be the best way to wear it. I often thought of cutting it, but I remember my Dad saying girls should have long hair because it shows their femininity. Seeing as I was already in a career where there was no room for feminine looking cops, I thought I would hold on to what was left of my feminine side.

"Well, are you ready to go?"

"Yes, I sure am, and by the way, Ruby has already advised me to watch my step."

"Yes, and Ruby knows what she is talking about."

Ruby smiled and waved good-bye to us. Gunn opened the door to his truck and I stepped in. He walked around and hopped in. He had a big smile on his face that appeared almost smug. I looked at him and said, "Is there something I should know about or is there a joke you aren't telling me?"

"Sorry, Meg, no, not at all, I'm just thinking about how Sabella will feel when you walk through the door. You know she has no competition here, and I don't think she wants any." Well, on that note, I thought I would probably be in for quite the night.

As we drove down a beautiful winding road I looked out and could see some of the most beautiful land I had ever seen. The trees were spaced perfectly along the road. They looked like they were planted by hand. Beyond the trees was a meadow, as far as the eyes could see. The sweet smell of clover was radiating through the air. The meadow came to an end and opened up to a lake, so blue, you would have thought it was hand painted. Gunn looked over at me and said, "Beautiful, isn't it?" It was breathtaking. I opened my mouth to say so, and just then he quickly said, "Look over here." And there stood the most beautiful ranch I had ever seen. The entire land was surrounded by a white fence about three feet high. The trees and the flowers in the yard were vibrant with color. The long curved driveway that led up to the house was paved with cobblestone. The house in all its glory was gigantic and as Gunn had said earlier looked like a cathedral. Large white pillars stood tall beside the entranceway. Huge windows surrounded the house, so that nothing would go unseen. A veranda surrounded the entire house, with hanging baskets of radiant colored flowers. It was a picture all right, not one you would need a picture to remember. Gunn pulled up in front of the house. It was almost a shame to leave the vehicle parked there. You didn't want anything to ruin the picture in front of you. Quickly, the double doors swung open, and there stood Sabella welcoming us into her home. With outstretched arms, she quickly flung them around Gunn and softly placed a kiss on his cheek. You could tell he was rather embarrassed by the whole episode, but I could also tell that was her way.

"Come in. Jack is in the parlor, so please follow me, and we will join him."

The house was as stunning from the inside as it was the outside. Huge pillars with hand paintings all over them. A large glass table stood proudly in the foyer. Upon it was a vase, so full of fresh cut flowers that it appeared to be overfull. The smell from the flowers was so sweet that you felt you were still out in the meadow. Sabella had her arm around Gunn and pushed him along into the parlor. I followed closely behind them still trying to get a glimpse of everything around me. As we entered the room over in a far corner was a huge leather chair. The room being so big, you couldn't make out the face of the gentleman sitting on the other end of it. As he rose and took a few steps forward, you could see the face of a very worldly man. A very successful one at that. His white, perfectly cut hair stood out against his dark tanned skin. He wore a white, short sleeve, sports shirt with a perfect crease down each sleeve. But there was a sadness in his eyes that came through even behind the smile.

"Well, it is a pleasure to meet you, Meg. I've heard a lot about you, and you are as bright as the ray of sunshine that is outside today. Bill was right."

I couldn't imagine how he'd heard so much about me, seeing as I just had arrived today. And he knew my name. I guess either Bill must have run into him or Sabella had been actually paying attention after all.

"Yes, it is a pleasure to meet you, Mr. Wallberg."

"Oh, please call me Jack. "

"All right, Jack," and I reached out to shake his hand. What a strong and firm handshake he had.

"Gunn, it's nice to have you over again. There are a few things I would like to speak with you about, but not now. How about we go into the dining room and have our dinner? Come this way."

Jack led us down a long hallway, the floors made of marble and picture after picture hanging on the wall. I'm certainly no art collector, but I could tell that these weren't your average pictures purchased at your local hardware store. The ceilings were so high you could barely make out the pictures that were painted around them. A great deal of effort was put into building this home.

"Jack, your home is remarkable, I don't think I have ever been in a home this grand."

"Thank you, Meg. It was my grandfather's and his father's before that. We have maintained it as best we can. Hopefully, when the day comes and I no longer can, there will be someone here to keep the Wallberg estate going."

THE WALLBERG MURDERS

"I'm sure your family would be honored to carry on the family homestead."

"I have no other family!" He very abruptly said, "I had a son once, but he is dead."

"I'm sorry to here that, Jack" and I realized I would have to be careful about what I said from here on in. I didn't want to upset him any more than I already had.

Sabella quickly broke into the conversation by saying, "Well, here we are, Meg. You can sit over here, and Gunn you can sit over here by me."

The dining room was as grand as I imagined it would be. The table set perfectly with only the best china and crystal. The silver glistened as though it had diamonds wrapped all over it. The backs on the chairs were so high you felt like you were in Hamlet's castle. As we all sat down in our respective places, Jack asked, "Would you like some wine, Meg?"

"Oh, yes, please."

"It is from our own vineyards in the back. I hope you will enjoy it."

He slowly walked around the table and poured everyone a glass of the deepest, reddest wine I had ever seen. As expected, dinner was fabulous. A very silent but proper lady entered the room followed by two neatly dressed gentleman carrying silver platters with them. First, it was the appetizers, then the soup, a wonderful lobster bisque, and then, the finest Prime Rib roast I had ever eaten.

After we were finished eating, Jack rose from his chair and asked Gunn to join him in another room. I remained sitting at the table, waiting for an invite, which I did not receive. The men left the room and Sabella very intuitively said, "So, where are you from, and what brings you to Daywater?"

She appeared to be very sincere with her questions, but I was just about to answer her when she stood up and said, "Would you like some coffee?" Again, I was about to answer and was once again rudely interrupted with a story on how she was born and raised in Daywater, and planned on staying there for the rest of her days, which, in my opinion, were a lot. She didn't appear to be more then 30 years old, while on the other hand, Jack appeared to be in his late sixties. An unusual couple, but not surprising when looking at Sabella.

"Well, like everyone, I needed a change. I was tired of the rat

11

race and the fast pace life living in New York. I have only been here a day, and already I am wondering why I waited this long."

"Well, don't get too comfortable" said Sabella under her breath.

"Oh, why? Do you think I'll be leaving soon?"

Just then, Gunn and Jack walked into the dining room and invited us both to join them outside on the backyard patio. As the French doors opened, I could see the vibrant colored flowers and the most magnificent back yard imaginable. In the middle of the backyard stood the most magnificent oak tree I had ever seen. The shade from the tree covered the entire yard. Off to the side stood a covered gazebo that had been totally surrounded in screen. Jack noticed me looking at it and promptly said, " The bugs get real bad out here in the evenings. I don't like to be chased out of my own back yard, so I had the screen put around the gazebo. Now I can sit here as long as I wish and nothing will send me away."

"A very good idea. I would have done the same thing if it were mine." Gunn appeared to be a bit disturbed after his little meeting with Jack and seemed restless and in a hurry to go, so I thought I would help him out by saying, "Jack, if you don't mind, I am going to have to excuse myself. It has been a long day for me, and if you don't mind, Gunn, would you take me home?"

Gunn couldn't have gotten out of his chair any quicker. He held out his hand very delicately to Sabella and thanked her for the marvelous dinner and company. He then turned to Jack and firmly shook his hand and very quietly said something to him. I strained to hear what it was, but to no avail. Obviously it wasn't meant for me or Sabella to hear what their little secret was.

As we proceeded down the road back through the beautiful flora and fauna, I bravely asked Gunn, "So, what is going on back there? It seems as though Jack has a little problem that he needs you to solve. If I can, I would like to be of some help."

Gunn looked over at me, and you could almost see the anguish in his eyes as he spoke, "Jack wasn't totally honest with you back there, about his son I mean."

I watched him as he drove slowly down the road. It seemed as though he wanted to tell me what was bugging him, but was having a hard time doing so. Then with hesitation he said, "His son has been in prison for the last 15 years and is now eligible for parole. Jack is afraid he will be coming to Daywater if he is released."

"What was he put away for?"

"Murder in the second degree. In my opinion, it should have been murder one with the death penalty assigned to it. But him coming from a prominent family, the best lawyers were hired and courts were bought. He managed to only get 15 years. The family was not pleased with this until they began to have their own doubts of his innocence."

"Well, tell me, Gunn, what happened? Why is Jack Wallberg so afraid that his son might be coming back?"

There was a delay, and then he bravely spoke up, "His son's name is Francis, better known as Frank. He was 15 years old when he was put into jail. Tomorrow he will be 30 years old. I received a fax at the office today stating that he had been released on parole. He was a very evil young man back then, and I can't say as he has changed much. I pulled his files and found out what kind of an inmate he was. You might say a very bright one. He was on his best behavior at all times while in the pen, but both the guards and the Superintendent know better. They just couldn't catch him. Therefore, nothing bad on his reports. Even the psychiatric evaluation came out clean. Imagine that, a young man from the age of 13 through 15 killed over 25 people, and it wasn't until the last one that he actually slipped up enough that we caught him. And amazingly enough, it was here in Daywater, two weeks after I arrived. I'll never forget that investigation. I just hope that he steers clear of here as I don't believe he has been rehabilitated. Anyone who could do the heinous crimes that he has, can't possibly be rehabilitated. He should have been sentenced to death!"

On that note, I realized that he had pulled right in front of Ruby's, so I thanked him for the ride and said, "I'll see you tomorrow morning. What time do we start around here?"

"Well, about 8:00 is good enough."

"O.K. then, tomorrow at 8:00 it is."

chapter 2

Morning seemed to come very quickly. It was going to be another scorching hot day. There wasn't a breeze in the air. I got dressed and was on my way down the stairs thinking about what Sabella had said to me the night before about not getting too comfortable, when I met up with Ruby. She held out a cup of coffee for me and had me come and sit with her on the veranda. On the corner of the veranda was a little old table with two wicker chairs. On the table was a breakfast fit for a king.

"Ruby, you don't have to go to all this trouble for me" I said, my mouth watering at the time.

"Well, dear, you have to start your day off right and have a good breakfast. You may end up being busy today and not have time to eat again."

I couldn't imagine that happening, but it was a pleasure to have such a wholesome meal. During my life in New York, I was lucky to grab a day-old donut or bun in the office and the coffee was strong enough to knock you back a few steps. I finished up everything and thought I'd better go to the office and start my real first day on the job.

"We'll see you later, Ruby. Thank you again for breakfast."

And I proceeded down the street towards downtown. I thought I would walk to work everyday, as it was close enough that it seemed a waste of time to start the car. I had to walk through a small but very nice park to get to the office, and it seemed like it would be very beneficial to me to be able to unwind each day after work and enjoy the blossoms in bloom before I got home.

As I approached the main street, I could see Bill waving at me already and yelling across the street.

"Good morning Meg! Are you on your way to the office?"

"Yes, as a matter of fact, I am. It looks like it's going to be another beautiful day today. Well, I'll be seeing you around." And off I went towards the office. As I approached the Sheriff's office I could see both Gunn and Max sitting out front having a coffee and chatting on about something.

"Good morning, gentlemen."

"And good morning to you, Meg."

Both spoke at exactly the same time and then looked at each other and smiled. Max spoke up right away and told me to go and get myself a cup of coffee and come back out and have a seat. I went into the office and off to the side was a freshly brewed pot of coffee and some extra mugs stacked up. I poured myself a cup and proceeded outside to join the others.

"Well, Meg, it looks like you will be starting your job the same way that Gunn did when he first moved up here. I don't know what it is about me hiring city cops, but it seems every time I do, something comes up. Maybe that should tell me something." He chuckled and looked over at both Gunn and me. "Gunn tells me he told you a bit about his first couple of weeks here and how we ended up having to solve quite the series of murders over a two year period."

"Yes, it is hard to believe that something so horrible could happen in such a beautiful town as this."

The entire time that Max and I were conversing, Gunn appeared to be troubled. He had a lot on his mind and didn't seem to want to share it with us. He fiddled with a plastic stir stick, flipping it through his fingers over and over. Max looked over at him and with a great amount of support coming through his voice said, "You know that if he comes back, we will get this guy again."

No more was said for the next hour. We just sat there on the porch and drank our coffee. Time seemed to drag by very slowly. The sun was getting hotter by the minute. Lucky for me, short sleeved shirts were included with the uniform. The three of us sat there waving at the townspeople going by. The odd "Hey there" came out from Max. I felt like I was in a parade while on holidays. I thought to myself, "O.K., I am convinced. I have to get used to this." I also had to remember I needed this in my life. It was much too stressful before, and I wanted something different. This would be O.K., I knew it. Just then the phone rang. Max got up and said that he would get it. You could hear him on the phone speaking in a rather disgruntled tone. Max was not happy with where that conversation was going. You could hear him raise his voice, and tell the person on the other end of the phone to fax him what he could and that we would keep our eyes open. Then a loud slam of the phone and out he came.

"Well, our worst nightmare has come true. Frank Wallberg has been released on parole."

The look on Gunn's face wasn't surprise but rather anger and hostility. He stood up and walked away without saying a thing. Max looked down at the ground and then up at me.

"The Wallberg kid killed his wife and kid."

"Oh my God, I didn't know. So, that's why he has been so evasive over this subject."

"I'm sure that he is planning a course of action right now. He knows, as well as I do, that Frank Wallberg will be back here, and he won't waste any time doing it."

"We will have to warn the Wallbergs and let them know that he's out."

"Possibly you could go over there, Meg, and speak to Jack. I'll give you as much information as I have when it comes through the fax. I can't see it being all that much information other than when he was released."

"All right, I'll go, and let the Wallbergs know. By the sound of it, I should be very cautious in my approach."

"Yes, definitely, Jack is going to be upset when he hears this."

"Oh, Max, is there a patrol car I can use?"

As he laughed out loud, "Well, we aren't that backwoods. It's around back. Keys are in the top drawer of my desk."

I smiled and then left. I drove up the beautiful pathway once again to the Wallberg's thinking about what I was going to say. After all, I still didn't know too much about the case. I pulled up to the front doors of the mansion and shut off my car. It appeared as though there was absolutely no one around. I got out of the car and walked up to the door and rang the bell. You could hear the chimes of the doorbell echoing through the house. I waited, and no one came, so I reached over and pushed the bell again. Possibly they were out back in the garden, so I looked around and you could see a pathway made of cobblestone going around to the back of the house. It was beautiful. You could hear the birds singing and smell the sweet smell of flowers. I found myself feeling that I had died and gone to heaven. As I reached the end of the cobblestone path, my heart stopped. This wasn't heaven; it was hell and still burning. I could feel my heart pounding so hard I thought my chest would explode. Anxiety filled my body to the point where I thought I would pass out. My instincts triggered, and I ran over to the area the bodies were in. Hanging from the tallest oak tree was Sabella. Her body was limp. I knew she was gone. Over to the left of me was the clean looking, very well trained maid I had seen the day before, serving us that wonderful meal. She was tied to a nearby tree, with her throat slit wide open. To the left of me was one of the gardeners lying face down in the pool with a knife sticking out of his back. I looked back on the large deck that surrounded the house and there, tied to a chair, was Jack. His mouth was full of dirt and plants that he must have been planting prior to this outbreak of heinous activity. He was bound to a chair to ensure he watched the gruesome suffering of the people he cared most about. I ran over to him and quickly removed the dirt from his mouth. He was gasping for air and coughing uncontrollably. He tried to say something, and I told him not to speak. I scanned the area quickly and spotted a pitcher with something ice cold in it. I ran and grabbed it and put it to his mouth. He swirled the fluid around his mouth and spit it out, screaming at the same time, "He's back! It's him!" I very briefly surveyed the area to insure there was no one around. I ran into the house and called the station. Within seconds, Max and Gunn were in the back yard of the once beautiful garden of the Wallberg Mansion.

chapter 3

Max immediately took control of the situation. "Meg, call Doc Winters and have him come out and see to Jack." Without a word, I went inside to find a number for Doc Winters. Obviously Max had forgotten this was my second day in Daywater. A few minutes later, while I was searching a desk drawer for a phone list, Gunn walked in and gave me the number.

"Don't mind Max, he just wasn't thinking."

"Oh, I knew that."

I dialed the number Gunn had given me. Instantly, an elderly gentlemen picked up the call on the other end.

"Hello?"

"Is this Doctor Winters?"

"Yes it is, can I help you?"

"This is Constable King, we need you to come to the Wallberg's immediately"

"I'll be right there."

I hung up the phone and looked at Gunn. His eyes showed hatred like I have never seen before.

"Meg, I want you to circle the grounds for anything you can find. I'm sure you won't find anything, but we have to look."

"O.K., I'm going to start just outside the gate. Possibly the intruder watched the house for a while before he entered the premises."

"Good thinking, I'll look around here."

Jack was trying to tell Max what had happened just when Doc Winters showed up.

"What in the hell happened here?" The look on his face was total disbelief.

Max immediately warned him not to touch anything without asking first and to not say anything to anyone about what he seen here today. The doctor assured him that his main concern was Jack Wallberg, and he proceeded to check him over.

Max slowly walked up to the maid who was tied to the tree. Her eyes showed fear, and they sent shivers up his spine. There had been a struggle. You could see the bruises on her hands and the scrapes on her legs from being dragged across the patio. You could see that she had been tied to the tree before her throat was slit wide open.

I walked over to the big oak tree where Sabella hung by her neck. Her body was limp. Her hair covered her face, but you could see blood all over the front of her brightly colored spring dress. Max turned around and saw the gardener face down in the pool. When he looked up, he could see the doctor checking Jack's blood pressure.

Both Gunn and I returned at the same time. Gunn immediately said, "Did you find anything Meg?"

"No, not a thing," I answered.

"I didn't think you would find anything, but it was worth a shot."

Max quickly cut in and said, "Well, I think we will have to contact the FBI on this one. Make sure no word gets out on this. We'll have to leave the bodies until they get here. We don't want to disturb anything."

Eagerly Gunn piped up and said, "We should talk to Jack before they get here, find out what he did see, and maybe we can get a jump on the investigation."

"Good idea, Gunn. I'll go inside and make the call to the Feds, and you and Meg question Jack." As he walked towards the house he stopped and said, "And keep your eyes open, I'm sure he's here somewhere watching us."

That sent shivers up my spine. The thought of such an evil person lurking around in the bushes, probably watching me right now. It didn't matter how much of this you see in your career, it still seems to be a whole new experience of emotions and feelings that take over your body and soul. Gunn slowly walked towards Jack. I followed beside Gunn, again looking over the grounds to be sure he wasn't there.

The doctor yelled over to us, "Quick, get over here, we are losing him."

Well, I couldn't believe what was happening? Jack may have been through some stress and possibly some minor physical abuse, however, there were no cuts or wounds visible. Instantly both Gunn and I ran towards Jack, but it was too late. Jack Wallberg had died of a massive heart attack, obviously brought on by the torment he had suffered that afternoon. Our only witness was now dead.

Max heard the activity going on, and stepped outside to find Jack dead. "What happened Doc? I thought you had things under control?"

"I'm sorry Max, but this is a surprise to me too. I know Jack's been through a lot, but he was a strong man with no health problems. I guess his heart just couldn't take it. It gave out."

"Well, this is going to change things a little now, won't it?" He looked over at Gunn and me standing there in shock.

Gunn stepped forward, and in his usual matter of fact voice said, "Well, what did you expect? This was too easy. A houseful of people murdered in the middle of an afternoon, and to top it off, we have a witness alive who was there and saw it all. Isn't that just a little too convenient?"

Max turned his head and faced the house, "I just heard a car pull up at the front of the house. I'm going around to see who it is. It couldn't possibly be the Feds already, could it?"

I looked over at Gunn and he had a defeated look on his face. "Gunn, we are going to get this guy."

"Oh, I know we will. It's the time it will take to catch him, and the damage he'll do in the meantime. I've been around this block before, and a lot can and will happen before we find him."

There wasn't much more I could say at that point. You could hear the voices of people coming through the house. It sounded like an army full of men on a march to their destination. Max came through the door first. Following behind him was an investigative team from the Feds.

"Gunn, Meg, I'd like you to meet the captain in charge, Ray

Willard. He'll be taking over the investigation. I'd like you both to extend your assistance and expertise to Ray on this case. I'm going to head back to town to try and keep the curiosity down for now, I'll talk to you both later."

chapter 4

It was going to be a long day ahead of us. There was a lot of work to do, and Gunn and I would have to help in any way possible. I knew it was imperative that this case come to a close real quick. We basically stood back and watched the team move in and begin gathering evidence, if there was any that could be found.

The coroner's office arrived and began going over the bodies. I watched as they scraped under each nail, picked through each hair that was found on the body, took blood samples from the clothing and from each person. They carefully labeled each individual bag and placed it in a large case. As they completed each body search, the victim was taken from its current position and placed in a body bag. I watched them lower Sabella's body from that magnificent oak tree that shaded their yard so beautifully.

What a shame that such a picturesque tree could become a haunting memory. Her weak, limp body draped over the officer's shoulder, the once arrogant, snide, but very stunning lady was now gone.

I could hear one of the investigators tell everyone to hurry it up because it was going to be nightfall soon. I couldn't believe it. It was around 10:00 in the morning when I first came by and sure enough it was getting close to 7:00 in the evening. Wow, how the day had gone by. Gunn and I conducted a final sweep of the area to ensure nothing was missed. There wasn't so much as a match thrown on the ground. It was evident that everything and anything had been picked up and placed in a bag.

The team from the Feds were packing up their things and loading up their vehicles. The captain in charge, Ray, walked over to us and thanked us for the assistance and asked us to please keep in touch with him with anything that we might see or hear. Then he got into the van and drove away. It was just that easy—come in, look around, gather evidence, and leave.

"So, what now Gunn?"

"Well, Meg, I guess this is where we now have to do a little investigating on our own. Funny how that works. They come in, take what they can get, and leave us with nothing to go on other than gut feelings." I could see the concerned look on Gunn's face. Tonight, I was going to find out what was going on in that mind of his. I had a pretty good idea, but I wanted to hear it from him.

"Gunn, I was wondering if you would join me for dinner this evening over at Ruby's? I know she won't mind one bit, and I think we need to discuss the case and how we are going to handle it."

"You know, that is probably a good idea. I'm going to go home and clean up a bit, and I'll meet you over there in about half an hour."

"I'll see you then." I hopped in the car and drove to the boarding house to let Ruby know that she had an extra mouth to feed tonight. As I pulled up in front of the house, I could see Ruby rocking in her chair, enjoying the calm and peaceful night. I walked up the front walk, and she was already standing up and ready to go inside to start dinner.

"Wait, Ruby, I was wondering if you didn't mind me asking Gunn for dinner tonight?"

"Oh no, the more the merrier. I used to feed fifteen to twenty people in a sitting, so I think I can handle the two of you. I have already eaten so if you don't mind, I'll just go in and get things ready."

"Ruby, thank you so much. I really feel like I'm coming home when I come here."

"And that's the way I want you to feel" she said in her motherly way.

"I'm going to run up and have a quick shower. Gunn said he would be here in about a half an hour."

The cool water running over my head and down my body felt

like I was standing underneath a waterfall—fresh and invigorating. I wanted to stay there forever, but I had to hurry and get dressed, as my dinner guest was about to arrive any minute. I could hear Ruby talking to someone as I was getting dressed. She sounded very cheerful, and I could hear the laughter coming up the stairway as I walked down.

"Wow," said Gunn as he stood up from his chair. "You look terrific!" What was so different that all of a sudden he would notice what I looked like and make that comment.

I could feel the heat rise to my cheeks and tried to think of a witty comeback, however, Ruby was too fast for me. "Well, Gunn, where have you been these last couple of days, You must have too much on your mind not to have noticed just how beautiful Meg is."

"All right you two, that is enough. So I get out of uniform and put on a dress. Is that the big deal?"

Ruby began to laugh and added, "I think it is the hair."

I wore my hair up at all times while on the job. I didn't have enough time to put it up after my shower so I combed it and left it down. I guess some would say I had hair like a horse's mane. It was waist length and shiny black. The easiest way to manage it was to put it up, but it did look much nicer down. In an attempt to change the subject I quickly piped up and said, "So, what smells so good? I am absolutely starving." I looked over at Gunn and said, "Do you realize we haven't eaten a thing all day?"

Ruby piped up, "Yes, what have you two been up to? I expected Meg to come home for lunch but you didn't."

Gunn quickly stepped in, "Ruby, there has been a homicide in town, and it's probably going to get out by tomorrow morning."

"Oh, my God!" exclaimed Ruby, "Who is it?"

Again, Gunn stepped in, "It was the Wallbergs and their staff."

"Do you know who did it?"

"We have a pretty good idea, but we have to know for certain. After we gather all the evidence and take a few statements we will be that much closer to catching the killer."

I knew Gunn didn't want to say anything more to Ruby about this so I cut in, "Would you like me to set the table, Ruby?"

"Yes, that would be nice, the plates are over there."

I quickly set the table, and Gunn and I had a seat. Ruby brought out a meatloaf that smelled out of this world. She placed a bowl of mashed potatoes and a bowl of green beans on the table.

"Would you like some salad with that? It wouldn't take me anytime to whip one up?"

We both spoke at the same time, "No, thank you, this will be great." We looked at each other and smiled. When our heads went down to eat, not another word was spoken. I sat back in my chair and realized just how much I had eaten.

"Ruby, that was the best meatloaf I have ever had. Thank you so much for dinner."

"Yes, Ruby, it was delicious, Thank you"

"Both of you go outside on the veranda. I'll bring you a coffee."

So we rose out of our chairs and stepped outside. What a beautiful night it was. The sky was full of stars. They were like lights shining down from the heavens.

"Gunn, I'm happy I came out here. It is absolutely beautiful in Daywater."

"Yes, I felt the same way a couple of days after I was here too."

Just then Ruby brought us out a tray with two cups of coffee and two pieces of hot apple pie.

"Ruby, I don't know what I'm going to do. If I continue to live here, within a few weeks I won't be able to move from eating like this."

"Well, Meg, we'll have to keep you busy because this is one thing that Ruby is well known for—her cooking." Ruby stood back and smiled. She enjoyed every minute of it. "Well, if you and Gunn don't need anything else I think I am going to retire for the evening."

"No, that's fine, you go right ahead. If we need anything, I'll get it. Thank you again, Ruby. Good night"

"Good night, Ruby. Thank you for having me for dinner."

"No problem, Gunn. You know you are welcome anytime."

"Don't say that too loud because I might just take you up on it."

With a smile she quietly turned and walked into the house.

"You know, when I came to Daywater this was the first place I saw, and boy, I sure am happy it was."

"Well, if you would have stopped anywhere to ask where to stay, they would have sent you here anyway. Ruby is the best, and everyone in town respects her for that."

There was silence. We sat on the veranda and looked out into the night. I was tired. It had been a long day, but we had to discuss what was on Gunn's mind.

chapter 5

"Gunn, it's been a long day, but we have to discuss what happened here."

"Meg, it's a hard thing for me. When I moved up here with my family I had the same hopes of semi-retirement as you do. But like you, after just a few days on the job, and trying to settle in, there was a double homicide. It was my wife and child." The look on his face was total devastation.

"I am so sorry, Gunn."

"It's not your fault, there is nothing to be sorry about. I would love to forget about it and put it in the past, but it doesn't seem to happen that way. Even after we caught him and put him away, our justice system is such that he is once again a free man. Frank Wallberg free, walking the streets, after he did what he did. It's times like this that I would like to just throw in the towel and lay my badge down to rest. It doesn't seem fair but that is the way it is."

"So you think that this has been done by Frank Wallberg?"

"Without a doubt, but we have to prove it, and that will be the hard part."

"What has made such a bad person out of him, Gunn?"

"Some say it was his childhood upbringing; others say it was after his mother passed away, and Sabella moved in. She tried to take over the entire household and fill the shoes of his mother, and

Frank would not accept that at all. So they got off on the wrong foot, and they stayed that way. No one really knows what goes on behind closed doors, and I guess now, we never will know. While Frank was institutionalized, he underwent therapy, and they found him to be rehabilitated. Now isn't that a joke? Due to doctor/client privilege, I wasn't able to find out what they felt set him off. Now he is out, and back to finish the job."

"But, why your wife and child?"

"They were at the wrong place at the wrong time. My wife looked a lot like Sabella. I was considering buying the Wallberg's car. Jack told me to take the car that day and let my wife drive it around for the day to see if she liked it. So, I did. My wife, Judy was her name, was quite excited about the whole thing, and took our son for a little trip to Norbrook, which is about 30 miles outside of town. On her way there, according to a witness, a truck ran her off the road and left her and my son for dead. Now if that wasn't bad enough, our witness had to drive to town to get an ambulance and the police out there. I'm sure you've noticed, there aren't any cell phones out here. Well, by the time they returned, the car was in flames and my family dead. On the opposite side of the ditch was an empty gas can that was used to set the vehicle on fire. Our station was radioed, and Max and I went out there to investigate the accident, or I should say murder. As we got closer, I could still make out the size of the car and a million and one things rushed through my head. I started to think about what time Judy had left and where she would be at this moment and then my heart stopped beating. I didn't want to believe it, but I was right. I jumped out of the car and ran over to the vehicle. The fire department was already there trying to put out the flames. They were yelling for me to stay back.

"Max rushed up behind me and said, 'Gunn, they are gone.'

"At that instant, I didn't know what to do or say. I wanted it to be me in that car. Not Judy, not my son. The next thing I remember was waking up on my couch. I honestly don't recall when or how I left the scene or how I got home. Max was sitting in a chair across from me, just staring at me. I knew he understood what I had just gone through, and he didn't have to say anything. The only thing he did say is, 'Are you ready to go? Let's get this guy. And so we did.'"

Gunn needed to talk and get things off his chest, so I didn't interrupt, I just let him say what he had to say. There was silence, and I thought at this point I could break in and say, "So, that's when you caught the Wallberg kid?"

"Yes, and now he is out."

"Well, when are we going to get pictures of him because don't forget, I'm new here, and I have no idea what he looks like."

"Max has already ordered a file from the Pen. So, it should be here in the morning."

"Do you have reason to believe it's him again?"

"Oh, I know it is. His dad was very ashamed of him and wouldn't hire a lawyer or help him in any way. In court, his father publicly disowned him."

"By the look on Frank's face, he would seek revenge for being locked up."

"And you? Do you want revenge as well?"

There was no comment from Gunn. He just looked at me with an empty look in his eyes. I thought that maybe it was time to change the subject and just relax for the remainder of the evening. After all, there wouldn't be any relaxing over the next few weeks.

"Would you like a coffee, Gunn?"

"No, actually I think I will go home and retire for the evening. We are going to be busy tomorrow."

"Have a good night, and I'll meet you at the office in the morning."

Gunn rose from his chair and smiled at me. "By the way, you really do look nice."

Before I could even thank him for the compliment, he walked down the walkway and got into his car and drove away.

chapter 6

It was going to be another hot day out there. As I walked to my car, I turned and waved good-bye to Ruby. It was much too hot to have any breakfast this morning, and I was in a bit of a hurry to get to the office.

As I came around the corner towards the office, I could see that there were a lot more vehicles parked out front than there normally were. I got out of my car and walked into the office.

"Good morning, Meg. These people are here from the County Sheriff's Office to give us a hand with the investigation. You and Gunn can go over the files they have brought with them."

Max seemed to be in a very cheery mood this morning. You would have almost thought he was on to something and getting closer by the minute.

"Meg," said Gunn in a very assertive voice, "you wanted to see the picture of Frank Wallberg. It's right here and very recent."

I walked over to Gunn's desk and looked at the picture of the same man who showed up at Ruby's a few nights earlier.

"My God, Gunn, this is the same fellow who showed up at Ruby's looking for directions the other night."

"Well, why didn't Ruby say it was Frank Wallberg?"

You could tell by the look on Gunn's face that he was frustrated.

"She probably didn't recognize him, but she did say that he

looked familiar."

"Where was he headed for?"

"He was looking for Charlesville"

"O.K., that's a start. Meg come with me, and we'll take this picture with us. We'll go and talk to the people in Charlesville and see if anyone has seen him in the last few days."

It was a quiet drive to Charlesville. Amazingly enough, neither one of us spoke a word until we reached an intersection with a sign on it that read, "Charlesville 2 miles." Gunn pulled into the gas station and parked in front of the store. We both stepped outside and walked towards the door. The door swung open and an elderly gentlemen stepped outside with his hand outstretched to Gunn.

"Nice to see you again, Gunn. It's been a long time since you've been here"

"Nick, I'd like you to meet my new partner, Meg."

"Nice to meet you, Meg, welcome to Charlesville."

"It looks to be pretty quiet around here"

"Yes, not much happens in this little town." And he smiled. "Come on in, and I'll get you both a soda. On me, it's pretty hot out today. So, what brings you here, Gunn?"

"Nick, there has been a murder in town at the Wallberg's."

"When did this happen?"

"Yesterday, but we need to ask you some questions."

"I don't see too much around here, but you know I'll help you in anyway I can."

I pulled out the picture of Frank Wallberg and set it on the counter. "Have you seen this fellow here in the last three days or so?"

"No, sorry I haven't, but I have been out of town for the last two days, and I had my brother's son work the store for me while I was away. You know I just got back this morning."

Gunn quickly jumped in, "Where can I find your nephew, I have to ask him some questions."

"Actually, when I came back from the city, the store was locked up, and he was gone, so I am assuming he went back home. I'll tell you I was a little ticked at the fact he didn't wait for me to come back. I mean I may have lost a lot of business. These kids nowadays, they just don't seem to care about anything. My brother has had a lot of trouble with him, living in the city and all, he quit school and just bums around all day, so I had him come up here and stay with me for a while. There's not too much trouble a kid can get into here. I thought that for two days, I would have him show some responsibility and tend the store and gas station, but well, that's it for me trying."

Gunn quickly interrupted and said, "Nick, I need your brother's phone number and address, we have to talk to him. What is your nephew's name?"

"He was named after his father. Joseph Jr.—we call him Little Joe."

"O.K. then, if you can write it down for Meg, I'm going to have a look around outside."

"Sure, no problem, you look anywhere you want."

Gunn stepped outside and disappeared around the corner. "Nick, did little Joe leave any kind of note behind as to where he was going and why he didn't wait for you to return?"

"No, not a thing. In fact, he must have been in such a hurry that he left the back door unlocked. It's lucky I didn't get robbed."

"The back door unlocked? Can you show me where that is?"

"Sure, come this way."

Nick slowly made his way around the counter and through a doorway that led to the back room. I followed him closely and looked around for any clues that might have been left behind. The back door was open, and Gunn stood in the doorway examining what appeared to be scratches on the floor.

"Nick, what are these from?"

"I don't know. It had to have been done while I was away, because they sure weren't here when I left."

"Meg, have a look at this. What do you think could have made them?"

"It looks like some kind of rake marks."

No doubt I was puzzled, and it looked like Gunn was too, until he spoke up and said, "You're almost right, these marks have been made with an ice tong. The big ones that are used to carry the big blocks of ice needed in Nick's cooler."

Nick turned towards the cooler and mumbled something that neither one of us could hear.

"Nick, what was that?"

"Sorry, Gunn, I get so mad sometimes. I usually leave the tongs hanging by the cooler so that I don't lose them. I can see that they aren't hanging where I left them. I'm just going to check if

Little Joe used them and left them in the cooler instead of where they belong. I wasn't expecting an ice order until tomorrow so I don't know why he would need to use them."

Nick opened the cooler door where he kept a few things like sandwich meat, cheeses, bottles of juice, and pop, that kind of thing. He didn't have much of a variety of food in his store. It was more for the stop, fill up with gas, and pick up some milk to take home. He stepped inside and fell to his knees. In an instant, Gunn jumped from one end of the room right to the opening in the door. There in front of him was a corpse. It was little Joe. The tongs still clinging to his body.

"Nick, I'm sorry. Meg can you take Nick outside for some fresh air?"

It was obvious. Frank Wallberg was here and left his trademark behind. Another cold-blooded murder of an innocent kid. Where could he be? Gunn left the body in the cooler and came out to speak with Nick.

"I'll have to use your phone and have the coroner come out and determine the time of death. It may be hard because we don't know how long he was left in the cooler. The body is well preserved."

"Go ahead. When you are done, I'll have to call my brother and tell him the news."

It was so sad to look at Nick and try and understand what he was going through. On one hand, he had a troubled child he tried to convert into an upstanding young man, and it appeared as though he may have been succeeding. But then, on the other hand, his life was taken away from him without that second chance. I reached over and grabbed his arm to help him up and get him outside. We slowly walked over to the back door, and Gunn went to the front of the store to make his call.

"Nick, you will have to make a statement to me on exactly when you left for the few days, where you were, and when you returned."

"Why, am I a suspect?"

"Oh no, of course not. We just need to know what the time frame is and when this could have happened. It may have happened right after you left or as recently as just before you came back. We have a pretty good idea when Frank Wallberg came to Charlesville, so that will help too."

I could hear Gunn talking to Max and I heard him say that he thought it was probably Frank and that up to this point, we hadn't looked yet for any evidence, but that was next on the list. Then I heard the click of the phone and his heavy footsteps coming across the floor.

"Nick, you will have to close down the store, for today at least and maybe even tomorrow." Gunn spoke in a very assertive tone. Nick wasn't pleased to hear that because his business was his only livelihood. "Meg, maybe you can give Nick a ride home and then come straight back here. We better gather any evidence we can find. Seeing as we don't know yet when this happened, any evidence may already be gone. And Nick, you know, we will need a statement, so if you like, after you talk to your brother, just write up exactly what you remember over the last few days. Make sure you have the time and dates of when you left town and when you came back. And listen, I'm really sorry Nick about your nephew."

"I appreciate that Gunn," and he walked back to the front of the store and locked the door. He reached behind the counter and hit the switch to turn off the pumps, then he hung the "Closed" sign on the door. "I guess I'll hear from you later on today? And Meg, thanks, but I don't need a ride home, I've got my truck here, and I'd like to take it home."

Off he went with a slow shuffle of the feet across the old wooden floor. Gunn went out to the police car and pulled a large duffel bag out of the trunk. He brought it into the store and opened it up. He placed each article very carefully on the counter. He had a finger print kit, a can of iridescent spray used to illuminate blood stains of any kind, a camera, and a few other items that would be necessary to complete the investigation. You could tell he wasn't going to get pushed aside in this murder investigation like he was at the Wallberg's. Between us, we had enough experience to complete our own investigation and probably have a better chance at solving it quicker.

"Gunn, all you have to do is tell me what you would like me to do. I think we can get what we need before the coroner's office gets here."

"You bet, and we will. You can go and get the pictures. I'll take prints. I know it's a long shot, but I saw prints near the back door on that mirror. I'd like to see if in fact they are the killer's."

I walked to the back room and first took some shots of the back room. I took a picture of the closed cooler door and then opened it up. I took a picture entering the icy cold cooler and then once inside I took several shots of the body from different angles. This body was once alive and full of energy. Now it lay on the floor, curled up in a ball with a set of ice tongs stuck in it. That was it, the ice tongs!

"Gunn! There will be prints on the tongs!"

Gunn quickly entered the cooler, "You're right, and they will be well preserved, that's for sure! Don't touch anything, I have to get the bag."

He was like a kid in a candy store His excitement showed through. Maybe we had him! Gunn returned with a pair of rubber gloves on and a large zip lock bag.

"Did you get all the pictures you need?"

"Yes, I think I have enough."

He slowly bent down beside Little Joe and commenced taking off the ice tongs. He carefully opened the tongs and slipped them into the bag, sealing it quickly.

"This will go to the Sheriff's office for prints, they have better equipment there, and it will be a lot quicker."

He marked the bag "Exhibit 1." We stepped outside the cooler and closed the door. In all of the excitement over the tongs, he looked at me and smiled, " Boy, I'm sure not thinking straight." He opened the door again bent down on the floor and proceeded to take scrapings from underneath Little Joe's fingernails. I took some shots of the back room from different angles. It was important to capture whatever I could and not miss a thing. There were many cases in the past where a crime was solved solely on the pictures taken at the scene of the crime. It's amazing what the human eye will miss, but a photograph won't.

I stepped outside the back door and took some pictures of the area around the store. There was a tree line about 40 feet back. I could see a shed tucked away in the bush. I walked towards the shed and looked around. I could see tracks leading in and out of the shed. To the side of the shed were tire tracks so I got some pictures of both the tire tracks and the footprints. It was easy enough to find out the size of the foot and whether or not it was Nick's or Little Joe's. I called Gunn, and he came to the door.

"Yes? Is there something you need a hand with?"

"There are some tire tracks here and some footprints. I got some pictures, but I thought you might want to cast them?"

"Good thinking, Meg, I'll get my bag."

I looked around to see where the footprints led and could see that they went straight towards the storage shed. The prints were very odd looking. You could see that the left shoe had a deep cut in the sole. Possibly it would help us to catch the killer. I looked inside the window on the side but couldn't see a thing. The windows were covered with old newspapers. I came back to the front and tried the door. It was open, so I turned the handle and opened it up. You could smell the mothballs and the dust immediately. It wasn't a shed that was used too often by Old Nick. I stepped inside, but it was dark. I stumbled over to the window and ripped off some of the newspaper. The light shone in through the window and lit up the entire shed. Although it appeared as though no one had been inside in the last year, you could see that someone did in fact go in and there was a great possibility that the same individual stayed there for a while. There were pop cans and food wrappers strewn around. An old blanket was in a corner with a jacket rolled up into a ball on top of it. I positioned the camera and was about to take a picture when, "Hey, what did you find?" I must have jumped three feet into the air. I was startled to the point of letting out a little screech. "I'm sorry I didn't mean to scare you," said Gunn with a chuckle.

"Well, you did a good job of it." And I smiled. "It looks like someone was staying here. Do you think it might be the killer?"

"Oh probably but we'll have to ask Nick when the last time he was in here, or possibly his nephew."

"I'll make a note of that and when we go to pick up his statement I'll ask him." I continued taking some pictures and then stepped outside. "Gunn, do you think that this murder and the Wallberg's are related?"

"Yes, I would think so. It is too coincidental that we would have two murder sites within a day or so unless they are by the same killer. The kid got in his way. Lucky for Nick he was out of town, too bad for Little Joe."

"Gunn, you have solved a case in the past with Frank Wallberg. Does this look like something he would do? I mean, we have no connection at this point. All we know is that he is out of prison, he asked for directions to get here, and he could possibly be on a revenge kick."

"I don't know, Meg. My gut feeling says that it is Frank Wallberg and at this point that is all we have to go on. I'm going to give Max a call and see how they are making out in town. Call me if you find anything else."

I nodded to him and walked around the shed one more time. I couldn't see anything, so I met Gunn at the car and got in.

"Did you lock up the store?"

"Yes, she's all locked up. I just talked to Max, and he said that the Crime unit was still there setting up shop. It looks like they could be there for a while. Max knows how I feel about those guys, so he told us to spend the day following up on any lead we come across."

"Sounds good to me. I guess we better go to Nick's and pick up his statement and ask him a few more questions."

His house wasn't very far at all from the store so we were there before I could even give my feet a rest. We got out of the car and walked up the stairs to his house. Nick met us at the door, "I heard the two of you coming up the stairs. Can I get you something to drink? Maybe a soda?"

Both of us answered at the same time, "Yes, thank you, that would be great."

"O.K. then, come on inside."

So we walked in and as I looked around, you could tell that Nick had lived on his own for quite some time. There were newspapers stacked to the ceiling, and pop cans overflowing out of a box he had in a corner. He must have caught me looking around because he quickly excused the mess and brought us both a soda.

"So, have you found anything yet?"

"No, but we did pick up some tire tracks and some foot prints. There are a few questions we want to ask you though."

"Sure, anything"

Gunn took the lead and asked him about the shed out back of the store. "When was the last time you have been in that old storage shed out back of the store?"

"Well, I can honestly say a couple of years."

"Has Little Joe been back there?"

"Can't say as he has. No reason to. It's been empty for some time now. I'm sure it makes a good house for the rodents out here."

"Someone has been inside there within the last few days, and I think it just might be our killer. Do you have a pair of Little Joe's shoes kicking around and a pair of yours. We need to know the size and possibly the prints on the soles."

"Sure, help yourself, all the shoes I own and Little Joe's are in the closet at the door. The only pair that would be missing are the ones on his feet."

"There's a mark on the sole of the shoe that we are looking for. I would think that it will be easy to identify."

I stood up and added, "If you don't mind, Nick, I'll have a look right now."

I walked over to the closet and opened the door. Inside was a large apple crate full of shoes. Again you could tell by the aroma that there weren't any ladies' shoes kicking around in that box. I pulled them out one at a time and flipped them over to view the soles. After about twelve pairs of shoes and boots, I came up empty handed.

I placed the shoes back in the box, trying to organize them the best I could, and closed the door.

"No, none of your shoes match the prints we found. Would you mind if I have a look around the house? There might be a pair of shoes that Little Joe left under the bed or something."

Nick seemed uneasy, but in a rather defensive manner said, "Yes, I guess it's O.K.. But what's going on here? Am I under investigation?"

Gunn immediately spoke up and said, "No, not at all, Nick. We just have to know if Little Joe was the one that left the prints behind. You know how kids are. They are curious and like to snoop around. If it was him in there, well, we don't want to waste anymore time thinking that the killer may have been staying in your shed and keep looking for something that isn't there. You know what I mean?"

"Yes, go ahead. This whole thing is making me edgy. Hard to believe, eh?"

Nick held his head down and shook it with disbelief. He probably was enjoying Little Joe staying with him. After all, he had no one else to visit with. I walked from room to room in the house and came up empty handed.

"Well, Gunn, there isn't anything else here that we need at this point. Did you get the statement from Nick?"

Nick stood up and walked over to the kitchen counter where he had a writing pad and paper. He picked it up and handed it to me.

"Here you go. I think this is what you are looking for."

I briefly looked it over and said, "Thank you, Nick. If there is anything missing that we need to know, we'll give you a call."

Gunn stood up and walked towards the door. He turned and looked at Nick, "I'm sorry, Nick, we'll do what we can to find him."

With a nod from Nick, Gunn and I left the house. On the way back to town, we both were quiet. I'm sure he was thinking the same thing I was—where do we go from here? I read over Nick's statement and couldn't find anything missing, so I sat back to enjoy the fresh summer air while Gunn made his way down the dusty old roads..

chapter 7

It was hot, and I was hungry. "Gunn, how about we stop somewhere for a bite to eat? I'm really hungry."

Gunn looked at his watch and instantly spoke up, "Sounds great. I could use something too. I never realized what time it was." Time seemed to fly over the last two days. It seemed like just shortly after you woke up, it was time to go back to bed. Gunn turned down an old road and pointed straight ahead. "Just over the top of that hill is one of the finest little restaurants you'll probably ever eat at. Funny thing stuck out here in the middle of nowhere. Some Canadians moved up here and started up this restaurant in an old barn. They worked on the barn for probably a year before it was ready to open. But now that it is, I can guarantee you that people come for miles around to eat here at least once a week. I know I do." He chuckled. Sure enough he was on the top of the hill, and right at the bottom was this old barn that was in fact converted into a restaurant. You could see three cars parked out front.

"You see, and it's busy again," and then he broke out laughing.

I could smell the food before I even got out of the car.

"Wow, it sure smells good here"

"You bet, but wait until you try something."

So we walked inside, and it was a picture of a quaint little restaurant. There were tables set for two, all over the main room. Each table had a vase with a flower in it. A candle lit up each table. How nice I thought, for a place so out of the way. It was owned and operated by a husband and wife from Canada. They greeted us with open arms and asked us where we would like to be seated. Gunn smiled and pointed over to the table by the window. And off we went. Gunn pulled out the chair for me and I sat down. The lady placed a menu in front of me, and one in front of Gunn. I looked at the various items listed on the menu and wondered what I was going to have. Gunn looked at his watch again and said, "How about I order today and next time I bring you here, it will be when we are not on duty, and we can have a drink?"

"Sounds good to me because, to be honest, I don't know what I want."

The owner came back with a pad and paper, and Gunn ordered the special with two salads and two ice teas. That sounded good enough for me, and I asked him what was next.

"I wanted to stop by the Wallberg's on the way back. You know if there is a connection, possibly we can find a print to match the one at Nick's store."

"It's worth a try. I think we should go before it gets too dark."

"Oh, there will be a lot of time after we eat. The sun stays up a long time around here you know."

Our salads were brought to us, and we ate. There was no more discussion from this point until the salads were gone.

"That salad was very good."

"I know. I always order the salad. She makes her own house dressing, and it's the best I ever had."

Then came dinner. I never did think to ask what the special was, but when it showed up, I was happy I left it up to Gunn to order. It was roasted chicken with all the fixings. The chicken was golden brown and steaming. The dressing smelled of herbs and spices. The potatoes were whipped to perfection. This was a dinner.

After we finished eating Gunn stood up and said, "I'll get the bill, and if you could, would you radio Max and let him know we are going to stop by the Wallberg's to have another look around."

Off I went to the car to radio Max. I was pretty full from dinner, and I was ready to have a little nap, but we still had work to do. I called in and spoke to Max. He told me that the investigation team hadn't put anything together yet on the Wallberg murders and asked how we had made out. I gave him a brief description of our day and told him we would be by the office at the end of the day. Gunn got into the car and we drove away.

"Gunn that was the best dinner I have had in years. Thank you so much"

"That's good, I knew you would like it. But remember, don't say that too loudly or Ruby might hear you, and she won't be too happy knowing she has competition out here." He chuckled and I finally broke down and chuckled along with him.

We proceeded down the dusty roads headed to the Wallberg's. When we reached the entranceway to the Wallberg property, Gunn stopped the car and turned it off. He sat in the car scanning the yard for any clues that might have been missed. Unfortunately with all the Feds that came out, if there were any tracks that might have matched the ones we found at Nick's store, they would be ruined by now. Gunn started the car again and slowly drove up the driveway towards the house. I kept my eyes on the shrubs that surrounded the property looking for anything that might not belong there. But nothing. Gunn stopped the car in front of the mansion and got out.

"I think we should have another look around the house, both inside and out."

"O.K., where do you want to start?"

"Let's go inside and see if anything has been disturbed since we were last here."

Gunn had a key to get inside and stuck it into the door. The door opened wide. Silence filled the air. We stepped inside and glanced around the room.

"Meg, you have a look upstairs, and see if you can find anything. I'll have a look down here."

I walked up the spiral staircase, and when I reached the top, I looked down. It was a beautiful view of the foyer. The flowers that were sitting on the table at the entrance were drooping. No one was there to replace them. I walked down the hallway, and I went from room to room to see if there was anything that might not belong. But again, everything was in its place the way I knew it would be. I came back downstairs and found Gunn standing in front of the french doors that led out to the back yard. He just stood there staring out the window.

"Gunn, have you found anything? There was nothing upstairs from what I could see."

"No, not yet, but I haven't finished checking the main floor."

"Gunn, I'm going to look in the kitchen while you finish up in here."

"O.K., that would be good."

And I wandered off down the hallway through the foyer and into the kitchen. It was the largest kitchen I had ever seen. It was out of a catalogue. The brass pots suspended from the ceiling, a herb garden growing in the window,. White floors, cupboards, and counter tops. It was stunning. I walked over to the large island in the middle and thought it was odd to see some food just sitting there. I called Gunn to have him come and see what he thought. With everything so perfect throughout the house I couldn't imagine that food would have been left out.

"What did you find there Meg?"

"This food. Doesn't it seem strange to you that there would be half a roasted chicken sitting here on the counter and an open bag of bread? I don't know, but anyone who keeps a kitchen and entire house this clean, wouldn't leave this food out here. And if you recall, there was no lunch served to the Wallbergs when we found them. I think someone has been here helping themselves."

"I think you're right, Meg. Someone has been here. We better have a closer look around, because he had to leave something behind."

So we proceeded to comb the entire house for something, anything, that would help us catch this guy. There was nothing other than the food left out on the counter.

"Did you check the food? If it was left there since the murders it would be pretty raunchy by now."

"No, I'll go back and have another look."

I walked up to the island and placed my hand on the chicken. It was cold. Too cold to have been sitting out there for very long. I reached inside the bag and the bread was still fresh. It would have dried up by now if it had been sitting there this long with the bag left open. Someone had just been here before we arrived. In fact, he could still be there right now. A chill ran up my spine at the thought of what could happen next.

"Hey! What have you found?"

I jumped back and placed my hand on my holster. Gunn looked at me and apologized for startling me.

"Gunn, someone has just been here. This chicken is cold, and the bread is fresh. I would say he might even still be around."

"Let me have a look. I'll know how long this food has been here for."

He reached over and placed his hand on the chicken and then squeezed the bread.

"You're right. This has been left out no more than half an hour. Let's have a look outside."

We walked back into the den and through the french doors which led out to the back yard patio. The once beautiful yard was not so beautiful anymore. The flowerbeds had been trampled. And there was a chill in the air that seemed to permeate throughout the grounds. We spread out to have just one more look around, but nothing. Empty handed again. I know we had to be missing something, but what was it?

chapter 8

We left the Wallberg's and were on our way back to town. There was silence for the entire drive back. The car came to a stop, and I realized that we were right in front of my place.

"See you tomorrow."

Gunn nodded his head, and he was gone.

The house was quiet. Ruby must have headed out somewhere. It felt good to come home to a quiet house, and not feel like you had to sit and visit with anyone. I wanted to have a nice warm bath and watch some TV. That was something I hadn't done since I arrived. I slowly made my way up the stairs and ran the bath. I went into my room, slipped out of my clothes, and put on a robe. That bath was going to feel so good. And it did. I slowly slid into the tub and just closed my eyes. I couldn't think of anything that would feel better than this did. The water was starting to cool. I guessed it was time to get out. I dried off, put on my robe, and went downstairs. A warm cup of hot chocolate would taste good, so I went to the kitchen and prepared a cup to take into the sitting room with me. I turned on the T.V. and flopped into the big armchair across the room. This was too good to be true. I must have fallen asleep within seconds. I could feel the warm sun on my face. I opened my eyes and looked up at the old cuckoo clock on the wall. My God, it was 6:45 a.m. I had slept there all night. Well, I felt rested and thought I would get dressed and head down to the station.

I enjoyed the walk to work each morning. It gave me a sense of solitude before I began my day.

I left the house and started my journey to work. Where was Ruby? I didn't know her well, but I think I knew her well enough to know, she wouldn't be gone overnight with me staying with her. Possibly she went in to the city for something. That would be an overnight trip, and she would be back sometime today. I'm sure I would see her tonight when I got off work.

I arrived at the office and found that I was the only one there. The door was left open, so I went in and made a pot of coffee. It sure was quiet, unlike my old office. I could hear someone coming up the stairs and in entered Gunn. He looked like he had been up all night.

"Good morning, would you like a cup of coffee?"

"Good morning, that sounds great, thank you."

"So where to now? It looks like you have been up all night thinking about the case?"

"You know, Meg, I really don't know what to say. I've gone over all our notes and the steps we have taken, and it's like we haven't done anything at all. I'm getting frustrated already and it's only the beginning."

"Something has to come up, Gunn. I think we should check with all the town people and see who saw the Wallbergs last, and what the conversations were. Maybe we can get a lead."

"You're probably right, everyone in town knows what happened now, so I think we can go ahead and interview everyone and then follow up on all leads."

Just then the phone rang and Gunn picked it up, "Gunn here, can I help you?"

There was no one on the other end of the line. I heard Gunn repeatedly say, "Hello, hello?" But nothing, just a dial tone.

The phone rang again.

"Let me get it this time."

I picked it up and said, "Meghan King here, can I help you?"

A voice on the other end of the phone muttered something that I couldn't make out. "Hello, I'm sorry but I can't hear you. Could you please repeat that?"

"I said I'm watching you, and when you get close, I'll see you."

The phone went dead. I looked up at Gunn and said, "It's the killer, he said he's watching me and that when I get close, he'll see me."

"Well, I guess we should have suspected that this was going to happen and prepared for it. I'll get the lines tapped immediately and in the meantime I'll check the recorder to see if I recognize the voice. Every call that comes in here is recorded. I also think that from here on in, you better stick close to me when investigating. He obviously has a shine for you and is going to watch your every move."

"I don't like the thought of that, but I guess it comes with the job."

I sat back in my chair and watched Gunn bring the equipment over to my desk and start setting things up. Max walked in the office and looked at us like he to had no idea about what to do next.

"Good morning, Max, Meg just got her first call from the killer, very brief but to the point."

Max looked over at me with a worried look on his face. "Are you O.K., Meg?"

"I'm just fine. But, let's get this guy, I don't take kindly to calls of this nature first thing in the morning. If he is watching my every move, then he is close by."

"You are right, Meg. Gunn, you'll now stick close to Meg. In fact if it's O.K. with both of you, I'd like Meg to move in with you Gunn. Just for the time being, of course."

"Not a problem, Max. When I'm done here we'll go over to Ruby's boarding house and move Meg's things over. I'm sure Ruby will be sorry to see you leave, but hopefully it will be for a short time only."

"You know, does Ruby go away at all to the city or possibly visit out of town?"

"Not that I know of. Why?"

"Well, she wasn't home last night, and when I woke up this morning, she still had not come home. I think it is odd that she wouldn't leave me a note or something."

"That is kind of strange, especially for Ruby. I don't think she has left this town in ages, not for any reason, especially when she has boarders. When we go over to get your things we'll have a look around."

Max went over to the fax machine, picked up the papers, and proceeded to look through them. Gunn was finishing up with the phone taps, and I thought I would go out for some air. I poured a fresh cup of coffee and walked out on the porch. I sat down in one of the big chairs and looked around. I couldn't help but feel like there were eyes on me. I didn't like it. We were going to catch this guy, and it had to be soon.

Gunn walked out and said, "Are you ready to go?"

"I'm ready, I'll just put my cup back inside, and then I'll meet you out back."

I waved goodbye to Max and went out the back door to the car. We quickly drove to Ruby's and Gunn shut off the car.

"You go and gather up your things, and I'm going to have a look around here. I don't like that this guy has been watching you."

"O.K., I'll call when I'm done here."

Gunn headed around the back and I went up the stairs to the front door. The door was unlocked, so Ruby was probably home.

"Hello? Ruby are you here?"

Nothing. No reply—just silence.

I walked upstairs and proceeded to pack up all of my things. Lucky for me I didn't have a lot. I scoured the bathroom for anything I may have left in there and checked my bedroom once again before bringing my bags downstairs. I thought for a moment and remembered that I hadn't packed my robe. I needed a robe living with a man, especially one I didn't know so well. Back up the stairs I went but it was nowhere around. I sat at the edge of my bed and thought about where I had left it this morning. I woke up in the chair, I went upstairs and got dressed in the bedroom. I dropped it at the side of my bed. But it was gone. I checked behind the door in the bathroom and in the closet in my bedroom. Nowhere. That was strange. I heard Gunn calling me from outside, so I thought I'd leave it for now and come back later. When I stepped outside Gunn was holding an old 2x4. There was blood on it.

"What is this? Where did you find it?"

"In Ruby's garage. I think we'll send it in for testing and see if we can't find out whose blood is on it."

Gunn carefully placed it in a bag and placed it in the trunk of the patrol car. He turned and looked at me, "Is that all you have? You certainly pack light now, don't you?"

"I have never been one to have a lot of things. I don't feel the need for two closets full of clothes."

Gunn placed my things in the back seat of the car and got in.

"So, does it look like Ruby's been home?"

"No, actually, it doesn't, but the funny thing is the door was unlocked, and now my robe is missing."

Gunn opened the car door and got out. He walked straight up to the front door, opened it and went inside. I hurried to catch up to him.

"If there's one thing I do know about Ruby, she wouldn't leave the door unlocked if she was going away for any length of time."

I followed Gunn as he walked from room to room on the main floor in the house. Nothing. He walked up the stairs and when he reached the first door he opened it and went inside. Again, nothing. He opened the closet, and it was empty. We proceeded to the next room—mine.

"This is my room, and I know there is nothing in there."

As though he didn't trust me for a moment, he opened it anyway and walked inside. He opened the closet and—nothing. I didn't have to say anything because he gave me a look that he was sorry for doubting me. The next room was Ruby's. He reached for the doorknob and turned it. The door was locked. That wasn't too surprising if she was leaving town for a few days. She wouldn't want anyone to go into her room and sort through her personal things. But Gunn stepped back and lowered his shoulder. With one quick push he broke the lock and the door flung open. The bed was neatly made. Her dresser was full of old pictures. Gunn opened the closet and her clothes were all hanging very neatly in order as though she had color-coded them or something. You could tell she was very meticulous because even her shoes were neatly lined up against the wall. On the top shelf in the closet was an overnight bag. Wouldn't she have taken this if she were planning on going anywhere over night? It seemed odd, and Gunn lowered the bag and placed it on the bed. He opened it up and found it to be empty. He seemed satisfied that there was nothing else in the room or anyone for that matter and walked across the hall to the last room. The door was open, and so we stepped inside. Empty except for a neatly made bed. The closet doors were open. There was nothing inside of here.

"Did you look in the kitchen for a note?"

I thought for a minute and said, "Actually, I didn't look for a note, but I was in the kitchen last night and this morning. I'm sure I would have seen something if it was there."

Gunn proceeded down the stairs and into the kitchen. There was a note in the middle of the table. Before he picked it up, he looked at me and said, "Don't touch it, but let's see what it says. In bold black print it read, "I can smell your sweet body on your robe."

Chills ran up my spine. "He had to be here after I left this morning. That's why I couldn't find my robe, he has it. My God! He probably sat and watched me sleep all night!"

Gunn looked at me and said, "Don't worry. He won't get that close to you ever again, I promise." I felt weak. What was I going to do? Do I stay here and let this killer torment me and stalk me? Or do I ask Max for time off and get away from here? He would probably follow me and then what? I was better off staying here with Gunn and help him solve this case just so that we could lock this guy up. I thought to myself how funny it is that all the training in the world doesn't help your inner fears when they involve yourself. If it was anyone else receiving notes and phone calls I would be able handle it. But it was me, and I didn't like that.

chapter 9

Every detail had to be considered. It was agreed that both Gunn and I would itemize every event for the Wallberg murders and for Little Joe's killer. We could compare the smallest of detail that we each noted. This sometimes helped to see something that you might have missed. We knew that the sooner we solved this case the better off we would be. This guy was going to play a game of cat and mouse with us. You could see it developing through the phone calls and now the note.

When we got to Gunn's, he showed me up to my room, and I dropped my bags inside. Down the hall, we went into a large study. There was a large desk with papers all over it. I could see that Gunn was working all night to solve these crimes.

Gunn sat behind his desk and began to make notes. I walked over to the window where there was a chair and card table. I sat down and began making my notes. For the first time since I arrived, there was no sun. Clouds covered the sky and the smell of rain was in the air. I went over each case separately. Although I believed that they were connected, there was no evidence to prove it. Could it be possible that there were two murders in this small town?

I looked over at Gunn to find that he was sitting back in his chair with his pen in his mouth. He was in deep thought. Then he looked over at me and said, "Meg, we have overlooked something, but what is it? Let's go."

And off we went. We drove along the winding road up to the Wallberg mansion once again. Gunn parked in front of the house and shut the car off. He just sat there for a minute and looked around. It was like a light bulb went on. You could see it all over his face. He jumped out of the car, and motioned for me to follow him. He walked over to the garage where Mr. Wallberg stored all his vehicles. Gunn had the master key to the entire premises, so he quickly unlocked the door to the entrance and reached inside to open the overhead doors. It was amazing. All three doors opened at once and I stepped inside. Gunn walked towards the back of the garage where there was a steep staircase to the attic. At the top of the stairs was a door. He immediately climbed the stairs and pulled out his master keys. He tried the key but it wouldn't unlock the door. He wasn't about to waste anytime on trying to pick the lock. He came back down the stairs and looked around for something to break his way in. Of course in a garage like this, you didn't find any tools laying around. I walked over to the workbench that was on the far side of the garage and opened the cabinet below. There was a jack and tire iron that would be perfect for the job. Gunn looked over at me and smiled. Up the stairs we went, and Gunn pried open the door. He stepped inside the room and yelled out, "YES!!!"

I walked into the room and there were TV surveillance screens covering the walls. They were still all on, and you could see every inch of the Wallberg estate both inside and out. We were finally getting somewhere. Beneath each screen was a video player. Gunn sat down at the large circular desk and began looking around for blank tapes. He opened a door and there were eight new, unopened tapes. I took the box of tapes and as he ejected the existing tapes, I passed him a new one to install into each machine. He held on to the tapes like they were gold. He looked around the room one more time and stood up. I looked at the video players to ensure they were still running. Funny how there were no cameras visible anywhere. Everything was running, so I followed Gunn out of the room. Gunn stopped and looked at the door. He had to fix the door and make it appear as though it hadn't been opened. The lock was broken and he didn't like the thought of leaving it open. I remembered seeing a tool shed at the side of the garage so I quickly walked outside and went to the shed. The door was locked. I turned to go back and get the master keys from Gunn. When I turned around to leave, there he stood. I jumped and let out a small startled yelp. He smiled and handed me the keys. Once inside I began opening drawers to see if there were any locks that we could install on the door. I found the locks and the tools that we needed. Gunn and I took what we needed and went back to the garage. Without saying a word, Gunn installed the lock, had the tools put away, and we were in the car and on our way back to Gunn's within minutes.

He pulled in front of his house and headed up the walk. I was right behind him. I wanted to see what was on those tapes. It was getting late, and I was hungry. I looked over at Gunn, and he must have been thinking the same thing. He opened the fridge and pulled out a large cooked roast. He set it on the counter and pulled out some fresh buns, mustard, butter, and a knife.

"Meg, it's not much, but it'll do."

"Gunn, I swear we think alike. I was getting hungry also. What do you have to drink?"

"Look in the fridge. If you want a beer, there is some in there; if not, there is a pitcher of ice tea. I'll have a beer." I too wanted a beer, so I pulled out two ice cold beers, and Gunn had the sandwiches already made. We went into the living room, and he set the food down on the coffee table. He turned on the T.V. and the VCR. We were going to spend the evening watching the surveillance tapes.

"Meg, I don't think we should tell anyone about the room and the tapes just yet. You know how it goes. The fewer people that know anything about this, the better off we'll be, plus we might be able to catch something else on tape in the meantime.

"I agree 100%. If the killer is still around, he might just go back there, and we could catch him on tape. Hopefully, he wasn't there when we were."

"Well, we will know if he was because tomorrow when we go back to see if there is any new footage, either the door will be locked as we left it or it will be open and the surveillance equipment destroyed."

I nodded, and Gunn put in the first tape.

chapter 10

We anxiously watched the video waiting for faces to appear. The video was dated for the day before the murders. It was the day we were there for supper. This would definitely help us in determining who was at the mansion prior to the murders. There was a lot of footage to go through. It seemed as though the cameras were operated on motion sensors only. This was good for us because otherwise there wouldn't have been enough tape. The first tape we were watching was of the grounds. We watched the gardener in the front flowerbeds clipping and shaping the beautiful hedges that surrounded the grounds. We watched the mailman come and drop off the mail at 10 a.m. We watched Sabella leave the grounds at 12 noon and then return at 1 p.m. When she came through the doorway, she had nothing in her hands. Where did she go? Then the camera switched to the back yard where Jack was walking through the yard with a paper in his hands and a pipe in his mouth. He was a handsome man. So distinguished, and yet he appeared so kind. He walked over and sat on his patio. The maid came out with a tray filled with coffee and cakes. She set it down and disappeared back into the house. It seemed to stay on one subject for no more than 30 seconds at a time. And then it would switch over to any other movement within the yard. The time being recorded on the screen was another helpful feature. We watched general yard maintenance and the odd appearance of Sabella and Jack. The camera switched to the front entrance, and there we were. Gunn and myself coming to have dinner with the Wallbergs. We continued to watch the video and noticed that it switched over to the back yard at about 8 p.m. You couldn't see anyone on video, but yet the camera pointed towards the shrubs that lined the back of the yard. Gunn paused the video quickly and we both looked at the entire picture to see what was there. But nothing. We would have to see it on better equipment then maybe we could zoom in on the shrubs. Gunn picked up a piece of paper and recorded the time of the film; this would make it easier for us to check it out tomorrow. We had to be in the house at the time however, getting ready to leave. Our whereabouts would be noted on the film that was used for the interior of the mansion. We would look at that one next and try to match up the times. The camera then flashed to the front of the house where you could see Gunn and I leaving. There appeared to be no other movement on the grounds for the balance of the evening until the camera flashed to the west side of the building. It was about 2 a.m. Along the shrubs you could see a figure. It was the shadow of what looked like a very big person. Who could it have been? It didn't match the description of Frank Wallberg. Isn't that who we were looking for? Gunn paused the video again and wrote down the time on his piece of paper. Another area to look at when we got to the station house. You could see the figure moving slowly along the tree line. The figure walked around to the back of the house and came out of the trees. Gunn paused the video, and we stared at the person. Neither one of us could make out who it was. Gunn began playing the video again to see if there were any better shots of this person. He walked up onto the deck and peered in through the patio windows. I was sure that once we had the video on better equipment, we could zoom in and make out who he was.

We continued watching the videos one after another into the wee hours of the morning. Each video had something or someone on it that had to be looked at in the office. Finally at about 2:00 in the morning, Gunn and I looked at each other, and Gunn shut the T.V. off, and we both headed up to bed. It was going to be a long day tomorrow, so we had to get some sleep. There were still a few videos we hadn't even looked at.

I crawled into bed and was on the verge of falling asleep when I thought to myself, I better stop in and let Ruby know where I am.

She is probably back from her little excursion and is wondering what has happened to me. I thought that I would do that first thing in the morning before I even went to the office.

Morning certainly came fast. My alarm went off and the sun was shining through the windows. It was 6 a.m., and I could hear Gunn downstairs. I got dressed and went down to find that there was a coffee waiting for me on the table and a plate full of bacon and eggs.

"Well, Gunn, I'm impressed, but you know you didn't have to do that."

"Hey, I have to eat, too, so what's a couple more eggs."

We both gobbled up our food, and when I was finished, I gathered up the plates and put them in the sink. Gunn looked over and said, "Let's leave them until after, I really want to have a look at the videos. I think Max is going to be pretty happy about this."

"Sure, but can we just stop by Ruby's for a minute, you know I never left her a note on where I'll be for the next few days, and I don't want her to worry."

"I'd like to come in, too and see where she has been, and I'd like to tell her to keep the doors and windows locked until we catch this guy."

Gunn walked over and picked up the videos and placed them in a bag. Off we went to Ruby's to see where she had been hiding.

We pulled up in front of the house, and it looked deserted. If Ruby was there, she would have had the screen door open, you would be able to smell fresh baked goods coming out of the house and chances are very good she would have been having a cup of coffee out on the deck. But nothing. The doors were all closed just as we had left them. Where was she? Gunn and I got out of the car and walked up the stairs to the house. The doors were locked, but I had my key with me, so I reached into my pocket, pulled out the key, and unlocked the door. As we stepped inside, you could feel a draft. It was cold inside. No one had been inside the house since we were there last. Where was Ruby? I was now worried, and by the look on Gunn's face, so was he. He walked around the house again to have one more look, and I went into the kitchen and wrote her a note telling her to call the station as soon as she got in. I didn't want to write down on paper where I was going to stay for the next few days. Even though it was a small town and people would find out soon, I just felt here was no reason to advertise.

"Well, Meg, I don't have a clue what has happened to Ruby but when we get to the house I'll make a few calls."

We locked up the house again and headed straight to the station house. Max was already there, and the coffee was on.

"Good morning, you two. So, how was your night?"

Gunn instantly piped up and said, "Max, you are never going to believe it. It was a real shot in the dark, but it came through."

"What is it?" Max remarked in a real curious voice.

"Meg and I went back to the Wallberg's last night, and we found the video surveillance camera room. We have the videos from the day before the murders up to and including yesterday. When we took out the film, we replaced it with new video tapes so that if anything is going on there right now, we'll have it all on tape."

"Good work! Is there anything up to this point? I'm sure you were up half the night looking at the tapes."

"As a matter of fact, there is, and I want to set up the video player here. At least this one allows us to zoom in on pictures. There is someone in the video, but to be honest Max, it's not Frank Wallberg."

"Well then, let's get it going, and see just who it is then."

Gunn quickly went to the back room and brought out the equipment. Max immediately told him to set it up in his office. He didn't want anyone to know that we had this evidence and in case someone walked into the station, they would be curious enough to have a look for themselves. So we carried everything into the office and set it all up. Gunn fast-forwarded the first tape to his first notation, which was 8 p.m. That was where the camera had switched over to the shrubs but nothing could be seen. He zoomed in on the shrubs and nothing. He began to play the video again and there it was, a beautiful doe feeding on the grass behind the shrubs. Gunn crossed off the notation and moved forward to 2 a.m. He slowly played the video to the point where you could see the person step out of the trees and come toward the back of the office. He paused the video and quickly zoomed in on the person. My God! It was Ruby! What was she doing at the Wallberg's at two in the morning? And on top of it, peeking into the patio doors. We all just stopped and looked at each other.

"Max, Ruby is missing. When Meg and I went there to pack up her things, she still hadn't been home from the day before. We stopped again today and looked through the house, and there is no sign of her. She has not been back to the house."

"Gunn, we better put out a bulletin to the other county offices. We have to find Ruby. It looks like she might just hold a key to some answers."

We continued looking through the videos that both Gunn and I had already looked at. Nothing. Gunn took the next tape, which was marked the day of the murders. Could this be the answer? Were we actually going to solve this case this easily? We all waited in anticipation waiting to see the footage of the back yard. The video flipped to the front of the house, and you could see Ruby walking up to the door. It was about 7:30 a.m. This was unbelievable! Who was she going to speak to, was it Sabella or Jack?

The door opened and out came Jack. He reached out his hand and shook hers gently. Jack then walked outside of the house, and they went for a stroll around the front driveway. You could see that there was a conversation going on between the two of them, but unfortunately until we found Ruby, we were not going to know what it was about. About ten minutes later, Ruby walked away down the driveway, and Jack came back to the house. The door closed behind him and that was it. Until 10 a.m. Jack went outside on the back patio with his coffee and paper, and the maid followed behind with a tray. Shortly after, Sabella came through the patio doors and sat next to Jack. The gardener was pruning the shrubs surrounding the yard and everything seemed to be going along as a normal day for the Wallberg's. Sabella left first. She walked back into the house at about 11:30 a.m. Jack stayed outside and lit his pipe one more time. He got up from his chair and walked around the yard. He walked over to the big oak tree and looked up at it. I'm sure he was proud because of its beauty. He then walked over to the gardener, and they spoke briefly. He turned around and walked back to the patio. He went inside the house and left the gardener to continue pruning the shrubs. The camera flashed over to the west side of the house again but you couldn't see anything. Not even a shadow. We paused the frame and zoomed in on the shrubs. Was it going to be another doe or was it going to be someone we knew. Nothing, whatever it was, left as fast as it came. The camera went black!!!

"Gunn what's going on?"

"I don't know Max, but it's not the machine. It looks like

possibly something went wrong with the camera."

We continued to wait and then like our prayers were answered, the camera turned on, and immediately flashed over to the patio. There was Jack! He had already been tied up to the chair. The time on the tape said 1:35 p.m. There was no one else around. Jack was struggling with the rope and yelling something. If only the video had sound.

The camera switched over to the far west side of the yard and you could see someone crouched down in the shrubs. Gunn paused the video and zoomed in on the picture. It was Little Joe! What was he doing there? Why didn't he help them? The camera flashed back at the patio and out came Sabella. She was being dragged by her hair across the patio kicking and swinging her arms frantically. Her mouth wide open yelling. My God this was horrible! But who was the man dragging her? He had the build of Frank Wallberg but his hair was light in color. Frank had dark black hair and eyes so dark they made you shiver when you made eye contact with him. He could have dyed his hair but we had to wait for him to turn and face the camera. Then we would know if it was him. Sabella fought him all the way to the big oak tree. He wrapped a rope around her neck, and she continued to fight him. She got away, she began to run but she tripped and fell face first onto the ground. The killer reached over and grabbed a potted plant. He raised the pot above his head and smashed it onto her head. She was out cold. The anxiety was building with all three of us watching this horrific video. We sat at the edge of our seats wanting to jump inside the screen and save what was left of Sabella. He grabbed onto the rope and dragged her back over to the tree. He threw one end of the rope over a large branch and began pulling it down. Her body was limp. She went up higher and higher into the tree as he pulled on the rope. Her hands hung by her side, and her head pulled tightly away from her shoulders. He fastened the rope to the bottom of the tree to hold her up in the air. And then he walked toward Jack. You could see Jack pleading with this person. He reached over and picked up a plant and some soil and started to stuff it into Jack's mouth. Jack coughed and choked. You could see his face turning color. Finally! He turned and faced the hidden camera. It wasn't Frank. Who was he?

Gunn reached over and paused the video. Max stood up.

"I don't know about you two, but I could surely use a breath of fresh air before we continue any further."

Like clock work, both Gunn and I stood up and walked out of the office. Max followed us out and waved us into the back room.

"Gunn, would you go and lock the door, please?"

Max reached into the lower shelf of a cupboard that was in the back room. He pulled out three glasses and a bottle of bourbon. He poured the bourbon into each of the glasses. Gunn came back into the room.

"I think that is exactly what I need right now."

Gunn reached over and picked up one of the glasses. He handed it over to me and then picked up another one. Max picked up the last glass and raised it in the air.

"To you, Jack. I'm sorry for what you had to go through." And he poured the entire glass down his throat. Gunn followed suit and drank all of his. I wasn't use to drinking straight bourbon at anytime, but I thought I better do the same. As I drank the bourbon, I could feel my throat warm up instantly. It was good. That is what we needed.

"Let's go outside for a bit. Some fresh air will do us some good. It's horrible to watch something like that knowing that it is over, and there is nothing you can do to help them."

We all walked outside and stood on the porch. The town was quiet. There was no one around.

"Gunn, Meg, we have to go through all of the tapes now. We have to see where this is leading. And what about Little Joe? Why was he there? What happened to him before he made it back to his uncle's store and you two found him dead?"

"Max we have a lot of tape to go through, but it's early. Should we be calling the Feds to let them know what we found?"

"I don't think we should just yet. I think we should watch all of the tapes and then ask their assistance in finding the killer. They have the best equipment and will be able to match his identity on the computer."

"O.K. then, let's get back in there."

Gunn was anxious to get back in and proceed with the videos.

We got back inside the office, and before Gunn started the video, he hit the print button and printed what was the best close-up picture of the killer we had at that point. Then the video went on. The camera switched over to the east side of the house. Around the corner came the gardener. The poor bastard had no idea what was going on and what was going to happen to him. The killer turned to him and with one quick flip of the wrist flung a large butcher knife and hit him right in the middle of his chest. He dropped to the ground. The killer walked over to him and picked him up. He put him over his shoulder, walked over to the pool and threw him in.

"Gunn! Where's the knife? When I got there and even after the Feds were through the entire crime scene, there was no knife."

"You're right! His prints are going to be on the knife!"

Max quickly announced that we will work on that later, but for now he said we needed to get through these tapes. The next horrible scene was the maid coming out of the house with her usual tray of goodies. When she saw Jack tied up in the chair, she screamed and dropped the tray. She turned to run inside, but the killer grabbed her from behind and with his left hand, slit her throat wide open. What a demented individual. Why? What connection did this person have to the Wallbergs? He grabbed the maid by her arm and pulled her over to a tree. He tied her up to the tree, but why? She was already dead and wasn't about to jump up and run away. That would be something for the shrinks to figure out.

The camera switched over to the front yard and picked up Little Joe. He was hiding around the planters and trying to make his way to the front entrance so he could get as far away as possible. It was obvious by the look on his face he had nothing to do with this. He was just at the wrong place at the wrong time. He disappeared into the shrubs at the front of the property.

The killer came around the side of the house and looked right over at the place where Little Joe went. He must have seen him or heard him. The killer ran over to the shrubs and disappeared into them. The camera switched back to the patio and picked up Jack struggling with the ropes. Then, as quick as can be, the camera switched back to the front and there I was pulling up to the mansion. The camera followed me up the stairs to the main entrance, back down again, and then followed me around the house. I remembered thinking what a beautiful day it was. And then the look of horror engulfed my face. You could see the panic and shock take over every inch of my body. Gunn turned off the video again.

"Well, I think we know what happens from here on in."

Max looked over at me and said, "Meg, I think you and Gunn should contact the Feds and have them get down here right away.

THE WALLBERG MURDERS

Fax them a copy of the picture you got of the killer and have them run it. Also, I think you should go back to Charlesville and see if possibly the knife is around there. You never know what you might find now. I'll continue to watch the videos, and if I find anything new, I'll radio you both right away."

Gunn called the Feds and was explaining what we had found. He wrote down the fax number on a piece of paper and slid it across the desk to me. I took the picture and faxed them a copy. It was going to be a long day.

chapter 11

We drove along the same dusty road we did last time. It seemed to be much quicker then before. We pulled up in front of the garage and Nick came out to greet us.

"Hey there, so how's everything with you two? Have you found out who killed my nephew?"

Gunn got out of the car and walked over to Nick, "I'm sorry, Nick, but nothing yet. We do have some leads though, and we would like to ask you some more questions."

"Sure anything, Gunn, I want the killer caught."

I got out of the car and asked Nick if I could have another look around. He nodded and in the store I went. Gunn talked to him outside and I went straight into the back room looking for the knife. If it was there, could we be lucky enough that Nick or someone else hadn't touched it? Hopefully, we were. I checked the counters and shelves. I looked under the cabinets and behind boxes. I opened the freezer door. I shuddered at the bitter cold air that touched my face. I could see Little Joe lying on the floor, frozen. I reached up and pulled the light switch. There was nothing in there. It looked as though it was cleaned right out. I stepped outside and closed the door behind me. I walked toward the back door and remembered that last time we were here, it looked like some one had been staying in the storage shed in the back. I would check there. I walked to the shed looking on the ground for any new clues, but nothing. When I reached the shed, I could hear Gunn coming out the back of the store.

"Did you find anything?"

"No, not yet, but I thought I would have a look in here."

"Sounds good, I'll help you get that door open."

Gunn pulled on the door, but it was stuck or maybe locked. Nick came out and yelled out to us to hold on, he would get the keys. Within minutes Nick was there with the keys and opened it up for us.

It was empty. Not even the chocolate bar wrappers that were there before.

"Gunn, I cleaned everything up after Little Joe. It was too hard, the memories and all. You know what I mean."

"Yes, I do, but did you happen to find anything other than garbage. Maybe a knife?"

"A knife? Heavens no, just the papers and garbage you saw."

"O.K. then, I guess that is it. If you come across anything at all that you think might help us, please call me."

"I'll do that."

Gunn and I walked back to the car and left Nick to lock up the shed.

On the way back into town, Gunn looked over at me and said, "What do you think? I mean about Nick cleaning everything up? That entire place looks like it hasn't been cleaned in years but now the freezer has been emptied and the shed in the back spotless."

"I thought it was odd myself, but if what he's saying is true, I can understand that."

"Well, maybe. I'm going to call Max and see how things are going at the station house. It's probably a zoo right now."

I sat back in my seat and thought about what he had said. And then I thought about the fact that Little Joe was at the Wallberg's and wondered why he was there. I guess we had to look a little deeper before we found that out. Gunn hung up the phone and said, "You hungry? It looks like Max stepped out for a bit."

"I'm starved."

"Well, how about we go back to the same restaurant I took you to before?"

"Sounds great."

And we were off again down the country roads.

63

It was getting dark outside already, so there wouldn't be too much time left to do any investigating. Gunn pulled into the restaurant and shut the car off. We stepped out and walked over to the door. But it was closed.

"In all the years I've been here this place has never been closed. What in the world is going on here?"

He looked into the windows and walked around back, and nothing. It was, in fact, closed.

"Gunn, if it has been open for all those years maybe they needed a day off?"

Gunn looked at me and started to laugh, "I guess you could be right. I never thought of it that way."

So we got back in the car and headed back to Daywater. When we reached town, Gunn wanted to drive by the station to see if anyone was there. The lights were all on, and Max's car was still there.

"Let's stop in and see what's happening."

We walked into the office, and Max was waving at us to come into his office.

"Well, we finished looking through all the tapes, and it looks like our killer has taken up residency in the Wallberg's home. He comes and goes every day. Lucky for us that you guys found the tapes before he did. The Feds are running his picture through the computers, but to be honest they are coming up empty handed so far. Any luck with the knife?"

"No not a thing. The funny thing was when I asked Nick if he or his nephew knew the Wallbergs he said no and that he had heard about the horrible thing that happened to them. But if they didn't know them, why was Little Joe there?"

"And Max, Gunn and I checked out the storage shed, and it has been cleaned spotless. Strange, seeing as the entire place hasn't been cleaned in years."

Max looked at me and then over to Gunn, "Why don't the both of you have a look at this file. It contains responses to all of your inquires that you found at the garage. The tire prints, that kind of stuff."

Gunn picked up the file, and we walked over to a table in the back of Max's office. We spread everything out and started to look at the information the Feds dug up for us. Maybe there were some answers in the file.

THE WALLBERG MURDERS

The first item in the files was the molds of the tire tracks we had taken from the shed at Nick's store. The response was that the tires were more than likely from a 1975 Ford half ton truck. The depth of the tracks indicated that the truck was empty. Relationship to the Wallberg's case—none. The next item was the shoe prints. The shoe was a size 10, heavily worn, possibly an old pair of Nike's. Relationship to the Wallberg's case—a match! The third item was the scrapings from underneath the victim's nails, relationship to the Wallberg's case—a match! Well, it was obvious that the killer in both cases was the same individual. That got Little Joe off the hook. Unfortunately, it cost him his life, but we know he had nothing to do with killing any of the Wallbergs or their help. I think Nick would be pleased to hear this. I think he had his doubts about Little Joe and this could put those doubts to rest. This was a big breakthrough, but it still didn't answer why Little Joe was there.

Max looked over at us, "So did you find anything?"

"Hell, yes!" Gunn was excited. "Max, it looks like the killer is the same for both crime scenes. He did the Wallbergs, and he did Little Joe. We still don't know why Little Joe was there, but I think we'll find the answer to that from Uncle Nick. We still don't know who the killer is, but I'm sure something will come up on the computer. The Feds must be running DNA right now with the scrapings they found under the nails of the victims. We know he is still going in and out of the Wallberg's, so we have to post some men out there 24/7."

"Gunn, the Feds have some of their men posted around the perimeter of the property. They'll see anyone coming in and out of there. As will the camera."

They have managed to position a man in the monitor room without anyone seeing so that end has been taken care of. There is only one thing …."

"What's that, Max?"

"Meg, would you excuse us for a minute?"

Now that was strange in the middle of a murder investigation. I get excused? Well, I was sure I'd find out soon what the big secret was. Five minutes later Gunn came out of the office and said, "Come on, Meg, we are going to get something to eat." And off we went. There was a small cafe in Daywater that we could go to.

"Gunn, I'd like to pick up the tab this time. Let's go over to the cafe here in town."

"The food isn't the greatest but it sounds O.K. to me."

We pulled up to the café and stepped out of the car. At least the lights were on and the place open. We walked in and grabbed a booth by the window. We could see most of main street including the station house. The waitress walked up to us and set the menus down in front of us.

"Would you like some coffee?"

We both raised our cups at the same time and then smiled.

"I'll leave you alone for a bit to look over the menu."

I opened it up, and there was my favorite—pork cutlets, mashed potatoes and gravy. I closed the menu and waited for Gunn to decide. The waitress came returned.

"Have you decided?"

"Yes, I would like the pork cutlets, mashed potatoes and gravy, please."

Gunn looked up and said, "I'll have the same."

He looked concerned. As soon as the waitress left I looked at him and said, "Gunn, what's wrong? What went on with Max?"

"Meg, Ruby is dead. They found her about 20 minutes outside of town in a broken down grainery."

"That is horrible! But why wouldn't Max tell me? I mean I stayed with her, and I liked her, but it's not like I would fall apart or anything"

"There's more to it. Inside the grainery was your robe, some pictures of you, and even a lock of your hair, or so we think. We want to test your hair with the hair found."

Shivers ran up and down my spine. "He has been hanging around that closely, and watching me?"

"The pictures of you are with your eyes closed, so it's easy to assume that you were sleeping at the time he took the pictures."

"But, why the obsession with me? I don't know this guy, nor have I ever seen him before."

"I don't know, Meg, but we'll find out. Max has put 24 hour surveillance on you. He's sure the guy is going to come to you again. The thing is though, if he wanted to kill you he could have done it already, so why the wait?"

The waitress showed up with our food. She placed it in front of us and asked if there was anything else we needed. I just shook my head and looked down at my plate. I wasn't so hungry anymore.

I could feel Gunn staring at me.

"Why are you staring?"

"I'm concerned for you, that's all"

"Well, don't be, there has to be a logical explanation for all of this."

I proceeded to slice my cutlets into small pieces and began to eat. Gunn followed suit. The food was very tasty, I thought, but not as good as Ruby's was. What a shame about Ruby. Why would anyone want to kill her, and how did she end up out there? That was just one more thing that we had to figure out. We finished eating and the waitress showed up with more coffee.

"Thank you, but none for me."

I wanted to be able to sleep tonight. I was physically and mentally exhausted. If I had another cup I would be up all night. Gunn must have felt the same way. He asked for the bill and before I even saw it, it was taken care of.

We got in the car and headed straight to Gunn's. It was a long day and we both needed some rest.

chapter 12

Mornings sure seemed to come fast around here. I could smell the aroma of fresh coffee. Nothing smelled better in the morning. I got up, went to the bathroom and washed up. I walked into the kitchen expecting to see Gunn there, but he was no where around. I poured myself a cup of coffee and sat down at the kitchen table. The daily paper was on the table so I flipped it open and started to read what was happening around the county. I could hear Gunn coming down the hall.

"Good morning."

"Good morning, Meg, I see you found the coffee."

"Yes, you must have been up early this morning."

"Why do you say that?"

"Well, you made the coffee, didn't you?"

"No, I just got up."

"Oh my God, he's been here."

I grabbed my cup and poured it down the drain. I took the pot and poured it out as well.

"That son of a bitch! In my house. What was he after? Let's grab a coffee at the station."

Gunn made a quick walk around the house, and we left. When we got to the station Max was there and by the look on our faces he immediately came over.

"What's the matter with you two?"

"That son of a bitch was in my house. He has crossed the line. Where in the hell is the surveillance that the Feds supposedly have on Meg?"

"Calm down, Gunn, they received a call this morning that there was some unusual activity at the Wallberg mansion so they all fled to the scene. When they got there, nothing was happening."

"So, in other words, he is on to us there, too. He's no dummy, and we are going to have to start being smarter than he is."

"Look, you guys. He seems to be drawn to me, so why don't we take advantage of the situation and set him up?"

"I won't go for that. It's way too risky."

"Max, I don't know about that. I think Meg is right. Let him come to us."

"Well, let me think about this for a bit. But for now, I'll let you both in on the findings from Ruby's murder."

Max proceeded to tell us about how the Feds were trying to piece together the fact that Ruby was at the Wallberg's on two occasions the day they died. They ran tests for us on the blood that was found on the old 2x4 in Ruby's garage and it came back positive. It was Ruby's blood. They can't understand why or how she got to that old grainery where we found her dead, but they were thinking that she was obviously going to meet someone there. Either Jack Wallberg, or was it the killer? Could it be that Ruby knew this person? We also knew that the killer was not finished yet, or he would have left by now. He's hanging around tormenting us and managing to stay one step ahead. But not for long. It would just be a matter of time before we caught him.

Ruby died quickly, so at least she didn't suffer. The coroner's office advised us she died from one quick blow to the head.

"Did Ruby have any family?"

"Yes, she had a son and a daughter. Both have moved away from here years ago. There was nothing for them here so they left to the city straight from school.

"Gunn, what did her daughter end up becoming? Wasn't she a social worker or something like that?"

"I don't know for sure, but I do remember her coming and spending a few weeks here with Ruby about a year ago. She kept a pretty low profile and didn't seem to get out too much. And for her son, well, I really don't know anything about what happened to him. All I know is that some time ago, probably about five years back, he got into some kind of trouble. I remember Ruby telling me she had to send some money up to him to help him out."

"Has anyone located them yet? I mean they are the next of kin."

Meg was curious now to see what Ruby's family was like.

"Well, Meg, they have located the daughter, and she is on her way up here, but they haven't been able to find her son yet. But they are still looking."

Just then the phone rang.

"Good morning, Daywater police service, Meghan King."

There was silence on the other end. "Hello? Hello?" Nothing and then I heard a click and then the dial tone. "There was no one there."

Max walked back into his office to go through his reports. Gunn sat at his desk and looked at the pictures the Feds took of the crime scene where Ruby was murdered. The phone rang again and I picked it up.

"Good morning, Meghan King."

"So, did you enjoy the coffee this morning?"

It was him. So I very quickly spoke up, "As a matter of fact I did enjoy the coffee this morning. Thank you for going out of your way."

Gunn spun around in his chair and looked directly at me. He picked up the phone at his desk and listened quietly.

"Anything for you, Meg, I was going to make you some breakfast, but I was running out of time."

"Well, why don't we meet for breakfast somewhere? I think we have a lot to talk about, don't we?" I was handling this conversation very calmly. I didn't want to lose him.

"Well, sorry, but I'm just a little busy this morning, so I won't be able to make it, but maybe another time."

"Well, how about tomorrow?"

"Sorry, I have to run, but I'll be in touch."

Before I could say anything else he was gone. Gunn tried to trace the call, but no luck. The equipment, being as old as it was, failed. All we could get out of it, was that he was just north of Daywater and within a 15-mile radius.

"Damn it!"

"That's O.K., Gunn, he'll call back."

Max came out of his office.

"I've already put in a call to the Feds, they will be here within an hour and set us up with the latest equipment. The lines will be tapped at the house and the station. If you can think of anywhere else he might call you, let me know and I'll have the line tapped as well."

This guy was quite comfortable with hanging around and taunting us. The only explanation was that he wanted to get caught, but he wasn't going to make it easy. Gunn walked over to a large map of the entire county that was posted on the wall. He took a red pen and circled the area he believed that the call was made from.

"Max, I think Meg and I should drive out here and have a look around. Within that northern 15 mile radius, there are only four farmhouses that I know of that are occupied. We'll go and interview all of them and see if anyone has seen anything."

"Good plan, I'll let the Feds know what's happened, and I'll play back the tape of Meg's conversation with our friend."

We were on the road again. It seemed like we were getting closer now to finding out who this guy was. That made me feel a lot better thinking that soon, this could be over and then maybe I could relax and enjoy my new job.

We drove along the countryside towards the first farmhouse. The air was so fresh. You could smell the clover in the fields. The sun was shining down on the crops and there was a breeze softly blowing through the trees. Another beautiful day. Gunn turned into a long driveway. At the end you could see an old farmhouse in dire need of paint. We pulled up in front of the house and out came the McGarveys.

"Hello there," Gunn shouted.

The old fellow came up to us with his hand held out. "Good morning, what brings you folks out here?"

"I'm sure you have heard about the Wallbergs?"

"Yes, what a shame. Old Jack was a good man. He helped everyone out here if you needed it."

Mrs. McGarvey turned and went into the house. What seemed like seconds, she came out with a tray of cups and fresh cinnamon buns. "Please come and have a seat." Both Gunn and I realized at that moment we hadn't had anything to eat yet and that coffee and fresh baked buns would be perfect. We sat down and had our coffee and buns. We listened to Mr. and Mrs. McGarvey talk about the crops this year and how good the weather had been for them. I looked over to the side of the house and you could tell by her garden that it was a plentiful year for them. Gunn and I sat and listened. It was obvious that no one had been around their farm in some time. All was well and that was good. The McGarveys were nice people and you didn't want anything to happen to them. Well, it was time to leave.

"Thank you for the delicious buns and coffee. It's exactly what we needed."

Gunn nodded his head in agreement and asked them to give us a call if they saw or heard anything that might be of help to us in our investigation. We were off to the next farm. Over to the left you could see a farm totally fenced with freshly painted white boards. The house had been freshly painted and it just glistened in the sunlight. We pulled up to the house but there was no one around. Gunn and I walked up to the door and knocked. There was no answer. Gunn walked around the back of the house and I followed him looking around into the yard for any sign of movement. I looked into the window and could only see a cat sleeping on the floor. He was stretched out in the sun. You could see that he was enjoying his day immensely. Gunn walked around to the side, and I knocked on the back door. It looked like no one was home so we would have to stop in on our way back to town. I walked around the other side of the house and met up with Gunn at the car.

"We can always stop by on the way back in."

"Yes, we'll do that. I'd like to get all the interviews done today if possible." We continued to stop in at all of the farms in the area, and we were lucky enough to speak to everyone. No one had seen anything out of the ordinary in the last few days.

We arrived at the last house before we planned to turn around and go back to the one house that was empty. We drove in and stepped out of the car. An elderly gentlemen came out of the house. As we walked up to the porch, Gunn smiled, "Hello there. How are you doing today?"

"Fine, just fine. What brings you here?"

"There has been some trouble in town at the Wallberg's, and we are here today to see if you have seen anything unusual or possibly any new faces around here?"

"No, I haven't. I haven't had the need to go into town for the past few days, and I've been at home the whole time. There hasn't been anything happening out here."

"It looks like we are hitting a brick wall, but I'd like you to keep your doors locked at night because we're afraid that the killer might still be out here somewhere. If you see anything I would appreciate if you would give us a call. Oh, and you know the farm about four miles outside Daywater, the one with the new white paint?"

"Yes, that's the Wilson's."

"Well, do you know if they have been around in the last few days?"

"No, actually they had a wedding to go to in McGillvery so they won't be back for at least another couple of days. They've been gone for a week already."

"Thanks a lot for your help."

Now we had to go back. That had to be where the call was made. We drove back the same roads we came on. You could see the white house from a distance. The property was well maintained. We got out of the car again and I walked up and tried the door. It was open. Gunn was edgy and he drew his service revolver. He motioned to me to stay behind him, and we entered the property. There was no one around. The cat stretched and stood up to greet us. He was definitely happy to see us. You could hear him purring from three feet away. We walked through the house, but there was no sign of anyone. There was a huge bowl of food and water on the kitchen floor. I looked around and spotted a window that had been partially left open, probably for the cat to get in and out of. I wrote down the phone number off the phone, and Gunn called Max on his radio. He quickly gave Max an overview of our day and proceeded to give him the phone number to check out. The Feds were still at the office, and Max asked us to wait there until they came and printed the place. We stepped outside to enjoy that fresh country air. In no time at all the cars pulled up and the investigators went in.

After about an hour they came out and nodded, " I think we got one, in fact we got a few, but there is one really clear print that was taken off the phone. We'll have it run as soon as we get back to town, and we should know within a few hours if there's a match to anyone."

I looked at my watch and it was already 4:30 in the afternoon. I couldn't believe how fast these days were going. Gunn drove straight to the station house and told me to wait in the car. He would be right back, and he was.

Gunn stopped at the grocery store and I waited in the car. Within minutes, he was back in the car. "I want to cook dinner tonight. I don't mind eating out, but I do like to cook too."

"I'm not much of a cook. I got used to the Chinese food restaurant across from my apartment."

"Well, Meg, I'm going to show you what a home cooked meal is all about tonight. If it's one thing my wife could do real good, it was cook, and she insisted on teaching me a few things. Which, by the way, I'm grateful for now." Gunn stopped in the driveway and hopped out of the car. He reached into the back seat and pulled out his groceries. I was looking forward to this.

"You know, Gunn, it's really nice that you are doing this for me, and I want you to know how much I appreciate this."

"Any time, Meg."

And he smiled. For the first time he looked like a little boy with not a care in the world. He unlocked the door and started to unpack the groceries.

"Can I help you with that?"

"No, but you can certainly grab a bottle of wine out of the fridge and pour us a couple of glasses. The corkscrew is in that drawer and the glasses are above the sink. Wait a minute, I think we should use the ones in the china cabinet."

"We don't have to, Gunn, any glass is fine."

"Oh no it's not. You have to drink wine out of a wine glass, my wife told me so."

We both chuckled, and I opened the wine and poured two glasses, and Gunn proceeded to chop up some vegetables. I sat at the counter and watched him prepare all of the food. He pulled out some chicken breasts and placed them in a pan.

"I think you'll really like this chicken. There's a fair amount of garlic in it, but it's real tasty."

He had the chicken ready to go and placed it in the oven. He had the vegetables in water on the stove and he pulled out a long loaf of bread. The smell of the bread made you think it had just been pulled out of the oven. I filled our glasses again and Gunn set the table.

"It's going to be about an hour, so let's go out and sit on the deck."

It was a beautiful evening, and I felt very relaxed.

"So, have you ever been married, Meg?"

"No, I guess I never found the time for anyone else in my life."

"You should always make the time for yourself and your personal life. You never know when it can come to an end."

I knew what he meant by that, so I let it go.

"Have you ever thought of moving back to the city?"

"No, I can't say as I have. I like it here. I came here for a reason, and that was to get away from the rat race."

"Don't you find that you get lonely?"

"I haven't yet and when you have investigations like this one going on, you don't have time to be lonely."

"I honestly can't wait until this is over. Funny, but I came here to get away from this sort of thing, and here I am right back in the middle of it."

"Meg, I can assure you, that once this is over it will be another five years before we come across this again."

"I sure do hope so. I mean it's still not as bad here as it was in the city, but I need a mental break, and it's not happening right now."

"It looks like you need some more wine."

Gunn got up and went into the house. I sat back in my chair and relaxed. Gunn returned with a new bottle and filled our glasses.

"The chicken is doing great. I've turned on the vegetables so dinner will be ready in about 20 minutes."

We both sat there and never said another word.

"Well, it has to be almost ready, we should go in, and I can do some fine tuning to the veggies."

He laughed and I smiled back at him. The aroma coming from the house was out of this world. I sat at the table and Gunn placed the food on the table. It was absolutely exquisite.

"You are right, it is the best dinner I think I have ever had. Thank you so much"

"Anytime. I really do enjoy cooking and especially when there is someone to cook for."

There was a loud crash coming from the back yard. We both jumped up, and Gunn ran outside. I followed right after him but there was nothing out there.

Gunn walked around the back yard looking around to see if there was anything left behind. I walked around the front of the house and I couldn't see anything unusual. I walked back around the house and I couldn't see Gunn. Where was he? I walked behind the garage and there he was lying on the ground face down.

"Gunn! Are you all right?"

chapter 13

I opened my eyes and looked around slowly. Where was I and how did I get here? You could smell the mold and dust throughout the room. I tried to get up, but I couldn't move. My hands were tied to the head of the bed and my feet to the foot. What was happening to me? I could hear someone in the next room talking, so I yelled, "Hey! Can you help me!"

There was no answer. It just got quiet. I continued to yell out loud to anyone to help me, but nothing. I could hear a door close and then a car starting. Whoever it was, was leaving. Was there only one of them? I wasn't going to wait and find out. The car was gone, and I was going to get out of here. I struggled with my hands, but the more I pulled, the tighter the rope got. This wasn't going to work. And then I thought of Gunn. My God, was he still alive, or had the intruder killed him? All I could think of was please, let him be alive and well. He had to find me.

*   *   *   *   *   *   *   *   *   *

Gunn lifted his head and had a hard time focusing on anything. He reached over and grabbed the side of the garage. Without any strength, he pulled himself up and started to walk towards the house. His legs felt like they were giving out, but he had to get to the house and check on Meghan. He walked inside and called out her name but there was no answer. The killer had taken her. He walked over to the counter and picked up the phone. His head was pounding. He reached over to pick up the phone and he found a note. "Yes, you're right, Gunn, I have her." He dialed the station and called Max, "Max, he's got her."

"Gunn, where are you?"

"At home."

"I'll be right there."

As soon as Gunn placed the phone on the receiver, he passed out onto the kitchen floor. He awoke to Max, holding his head and one of the Federal agents calling in the doctor.

"Max, don't worry about me, we have to find her. You know what he'll do to her."

"We are going to have you looked at first, I mean I need your help in finding her."

"What time is it?"

"It's 7:30."

"7:30 at night? It can't be."

"No, in the morning. You must have been out all night."

The doctor arrived and quickly checked him over. It was a minor concussion, but 24-hour bed rest was required. The doctor and Max walked him over to the sofa and laid him down.

"You are going to have to stay here and rest, we will have the Feds help out for now. I want you to tell me what happened here."

Gunn proceeded to give the events of the evening. The dinner, the loud bang, and the look around the yard. That was all he could remember.

"The next thing I knew, Max, I had a hell of a headache, and Meg was gone. Did you see the note on the counter by the phone?"

"Yes, we had a look at it, and the agent has taken it in to get it printed. We don't expect to find anything because everything else keeps coming up blank. This guy is using gloves, so he's not that stupid. But he will slip up, it's just a matter of time."

"Yes, but how much time do we have?"

Gunn's negative response concerned Max. It was better to stay positive at a time like this; it helped you to think more clearly.

"I'll let you rest for a while. I know you aren't going to stay here all day like you're suppose to. One of the agents is going to stay with you until you feel up to coming to the station and then we'll make a plan to get Meg back. If there is one good thing in all of this, he doesn't want to kill her or she would have been laying in the back yard with you."

Gunn tried to stand up to show that he was ready to go with Max, but he quickly sat down again.

"I guess my head needs a little time to clear out the cobwebs. I'll be down there in a couple hours."

One agent stayed behind and the rest went back to the station to proceed with a plan of action to get Meghan King back.

*   *   *   *   *   *   *   *   *   *

The room was hot. The air stifling. "I can't breathe in here! If anybody is there, please open a window!"

I couldn't hear anything. There must only be one and unfortunately for me, I think it was the wrong one. It has to be the killer. My God, what does he want with me? I kept trying to break free from the ties but no luck. I could feel the rope cutting into my wrists. They were beginning to hurt, and I had to stop pulling on them.

I heard a car pull up and the car door slam. Someone was back. "Hey, help me! I can't breathe in here! Let me out of here!"

The door opened and there stood my captor. "I guess it is hot in here. Let me get that window for you." He walked over and opened the window. Immediately I could feel the breeze blow over my body.

"Who are you? What do you want with me?"

"Now, now, enough questions, you'll find out soon enough." And he left the room.

"You know they will come looking for me! And they will find me!" I said that with hesitation. Would they find me soon or when it was too late? In all my training, I have learned that you have no more than a 24-hour window in which you must find the hostage. After that, it is usually too late. Maybe I could talk with this guy and get him to realize what a big mistake it was for him to take me hostage. He came back in with a tray of food. "You must be hungry?"

My first instinct was to say I wasn't, but I realized that this could be my chance for freedom. "Yes, actually I am, but how do you expect me to eat lying down, all tied up?"

"I can help you out there, but I'll tell you right now, if you try to escape, your friends will find you sooner than they would like to and they'll wish they never did."

He was very firm on that statement. I think I would wait with the escape attempt, and try to find out whatever I could about him. He set the tray on a box that was beside the window. He walked over to me and began to loosen the rope around my feet. He didn't untie it all the way he just lengthened the rope so I was able to sit up. He then walked over to me and untied my wrists. "You can sit up and eat."

He placed the tray on my lap and just the thought of eating at that moment made me feel sick. But I had to eat. I told him I was starved, and I didn't want him to lose trust in me. So, I looked at the tray and there was a sandwich wrapped up, there was an apple and a glass of orange juice.

"I hope this will be all right. I wasn't sure what you liked to eat."

"Oh, this will be fine, thank you. So tell me, who are you?"

"Let's just say I used to be a local, but now I'm just an admirer."

"An admirer? Of what?"

"You, of course. I came back to Daywater to get a job done. When I saw you, I found that I wasn't able to leave. Funny thing, eh?"

"Who put you up to this so called job?"

"Let's just say an acquaintance of mine."

"But why would you want to kill the Wallbergs?"

I thought I would try to get what I could while he was talking.

"They did someone I know wrong. They had to pay. Too bad about the other kid though."

"Who—Little Joe?"

"Yes, if that's what you call him. He just managed to get in the way. He saw a little too much, that Little Joe."

"What about Ruby? She hadn't hurt anyone."

"I didn't want that to happen, but it did. And I don't want to talk about this anymore."

You could tell that although he had killed Ruby, it made him feel bad for doing so. This was something I could use on him later. Hopefully, break through.

"I've had enough to eat, thanks. Why are you doing this to me?"

He turned and walked over to me. He picked up the tray and placed it on the box. I tried to look through the window in an attempt to try and figure out where I was. There was nothing but trees around the entire window. He walked over to the foot of the bed and tightened the rope on my feet. With him pulling the rope, it forced me to be in a prone position again. He then came up to my hands and tightened the rope around my wrists. He never said a word he just continued tightening the rope. He didn't want to make eye contact with me. Was it that he did truly have a soft spot for me? But, why me? This made no sense at all. He turned around picked up the tray and walked out of the room.

"Aren't you going to talk to me?"

No answer. The door opened and then closed, he was gone again. Where was he going? I couldn't hear the car start this time. He had to be outside doing something, but what? I realized now that I was in for the duration unless Gunn could find me. It was quiet and I strained to try and see something, anything to help me get out of this mess. It seemed like hours had gone by when I heard the door open again. He walked in to the room and stood in the doorway.

"What is your name? I think it's only fair you tell me yours because you already know mine."

"Ben, but it doesn't much matter."

"But it does matter, I like to know who it is I'm talking to." I thought that if I could get inside this guy I could probably make it out of here alive, whether I had help or not. "Ben, if you are an admirer of mine, then why did you go to all this trouble and tie me up here? What do you have in mind for me?"

"I wish you would stop asking so many questions. In time, you'll see. For now, there is something I have to do."

He reached into his pocket and pulled out a handkerchief. He walked up to me and tightly tied the handkerchief over my eyes.

"Are we going somewhere?"

No response from Ben. I heard him leave the room and a few minutes later walk back in. I was sure I heard another set of footsteps.

"Is they're someone else with you?"

Ben didn't respond, which meant that there was. What were they up to now?

"I have to leave for a while, but I'll be back soon."

"How long is soon? You can't leave me here by myself. Where will I get food and water?"

"You'll be taken care of don't worry."

THE WALLBERG MURDERS

I tried to move my head to see if I could see through the blindfold. I couldn't, it was just too tight. I heard the footsteps out of the room and then the door open. I tried to hear if there was any conversation and what it was about because I knew now that there was someone else there. I only heard mumbling of two people talking but couldn't make out what they were talking about. The car started and then drove away. There was silence.

chapter 14

By the time Gunn was able to move around freely, it was late in the afternoon. He had the agent drive him down to the station. When he walked in the door, Max looked at him and with anticipation in his voice said, "I'm happy to see you're up and around. We need your help on this badly." He walked over to his desk and sat down. He could see this was going to be painful. "Gunn we have run all of the prints we found at all of the crime scenes. There is a set of prints that have come up on the computer. They are registered to a Benjamin Gale. His last known address happens to be in your old neighborhood in New York."

"What? Are you saying I know him?"

"If we're lucky, yes, you know him."

"Do you have a picture on him yet?"

"As a matter of fact, we do. It's over here on the computer."

Gunn walked over to the table and looked at the picture in front of him. It was the killer, the same guy who was on the surveillance cameras at the Wallberg's.

"It's him, the killer. Well, at least we know we have him. We just have to find him."

"Do you know him?"

"I can't say as I do. Does he have a long rap sheet?"

"He sure does, but it's mostly drug related charges and a few break and enter. I have the Feds checking to see who was the officer in charge at the time of his busts."

"Man, being a cop in New York, you see so many people and bust so many, unless they have done something to you that permanently engraves their face into your mind, you just can't remember all of them. Of course, it doesn't help that I just got bashed in the head with something."

"Well, I think we have come a long way on this in a short time. I also know this will buy us some time."

"Why would you say that?"

"Well, because if I'm right on this, he doesn't want Meg, he really wants you."

"Slow down, what are you saying?"

Gunn was totally puzzled now. He couldn't seem to figure out what Max was talking about. Max looked at him and said, "Well, think about it. He lived in your neighborhood when you were a cop in New York. Chances are we are going to find out that you did bust him and put him away for a few years. The guy obviously didn't like his new place of residence for the past 15 years and is now out and on a mission to get the guy who put him there. Now all we have to figure out is why is he killing people around you, and why would he take Meg? For the purpose of driving you nuts? It doesn't make a lot of sense other than he is using her as bait to get you out there."

Gunn thought about what Max had just said, and it seemed feasible. This guy wanted me, therefore I had to make myself available or we wouldn't get Meg back.

"Max, what do you recommend? I mean, what should we do? I would like to get out there and have him come to me. But wait a minute, we are missing something here. He had the chance to take me when he hit me over the head and knocked me out. Instead he took Meg."

"I know. We have thought about that, but can't figure out a motive yet."

"So, let's do something! Every minute we waste is life or death to Meg."

"I know that."

Max looked very distraught. The lines on his forehead seemed to deepen. His eyes looked weary. He was at a loss for words.

"Max, I'm sorry. It's not your fault, but I'm getting frustrated. I think he's around here, and I think a lot closer than we know.

"Why don't we get all the help we can and start searching every house and every farm within a 30 mile radius."

"Gunn, that's a good idea."

Max looked over at the Federal agent who seemed to be around all the time and said, "What is your name anyway?"

"Agent James Moore."

"Well, Agent Moore, how many of your men can you round up within the next half hour? I would like every one you can to meet here at the station. Gunn and I'll put together a plan and fill you all in."

James nodded his head and out the door he went. Max looked over at Gunn, "Pretty bad eh? I didn't even know the guy's name."

They both chuckled. It was the first time they both had actually smiled in days. Max and Gunn walked over to the large map on the wall of the entire surrounding area. They marked off a thirty mile radius with a bright red pen and started to count the farms within the area. Although Meg and Gunn had been to all of them, they would go again and this time search each house personally. Within a half hour, the door opened and in came five Federal agents all ready for direction. Max laid out the game plan and handed out maps he had made and names of the property owners in the area. He also advised that each house was to be searched personally. In addition, each detective was to call the station upon entering the property and again call the station immediately after leaving it. They were to take down the names of the people interviewed and any visitors that may be staying with the owners.

"O.K. guys, let's get out there and find them. Remember, be careful because we know he's there, and he will try to get you before you can get him. And unless you see Meg, do not shoot to kill, or we may not find her. Here's a picture of Meg for those of you who haven't seen her. The flaming red hair is a dead giveaway, so don't make any mistakes. Good luck!"

They all marched out of the station, hopped in their cars, and they were gone. Gunn stayed in the station house until they left and then turned to Max, "Max, I think I want to check Ruby's again. For some reason I think we have missed something."

"Well, if you feel that strongly about it, go ahead and have another look, but this time be careful, I don't think you want another lump on the head, do you?"

Gunn just smiled at Max and left. He headed straight to Ruby's.

He thought to himself, "Why do I feel like there is a connection here? Is it because I saw Ruby on video at the Wallberg's?"

He walked up the sidewalk and stopped at the base of the stairs. Why were all the curtains closed? They weren't closed when we left there. Someone was either in the house or was there and left. He couldn't decide if he should call Max or just go on ahead and check things out first. It was quicker to just storm the house, and if he needed help, he could always call it in.

chapter 15

I lay in bed with a blindfold over my eyes. It was deathly hot in here, and it made me feel sick to my stomach. I could feel the perspiration running down the backs of my arms. I could feel a pool of sweat form between my breasts. I didn't like this feeling, and I was beginning to feel claustrophobic. I wanted this thing off my face and eyes. I yelled out as loud as I could, "Take this thing off! I know you are sitting there watching me, and I want this thing off!" I heard the most hideous laughter and then the door slammed shut. My skin crawled. For the first time, I was actually scared. I could handle Ben, but not this guy. How was I going to get out of here? I had to break free and take my chances. I pulled on my hands and my legs and struggled with the rope, but I couldn't budge them. I felt totally defeated. My body went limp, and I must have fallen asleep. I lay in bed, tied at the hands and feet, and slept soundly. It was the heat and the exhaustion that wiped me out.

I could smell a horrible smell, and then suddenly there was someone ripping at my clothes! My shirt was ripped wide open exposing my breasts. There were large, horrible, hands all over me, and I began to scream as loud as I could. No one was helping me! That hideous laughter started and then my pants were pulled down to my ankles. I wanted to die right there. I continued to scream, and he laughed harder. I wanted this to stop now! This couldn't happen to me! Please God, if you are out there, help me, help me now!!!

I heard the door swing open and slam against the wall. It was Ben! "Get away from her!" He yelled in a very assertive voice.

The man on top of me stopped grabbing me and in one quick turn, yelled back, "You just don't worry about this little filly, I'll take care of her."

I heard the click of a gun, and Ben very slowly said, "I told you to get away from her, and I mean right now!"

"Come on now, I was just having a little fun here."

"We don't have time for fun. We have to make a move so come outside, I have to talk to you."

My worst nightmare was over! I didn't think I would make it through this. Thank you, Ben, for coming back when you did. I strained to hear what was being said, but I could only hear mumbling sounds from the other room. I could hear someone walk across the other room and then the door opened and closed. Please Ben, don't leave me here again with this person, or I'm going to die literally. I knew that. I could hear the car start and speed off on the gravel driveway.

The door of my room opened. My heart began to pound so hard I thought I could hear it. I was going to have an anxiety attack! My chest tightened up, and I couldn't breath. I gasped for air and pulled on the ropes again. I had to break free! It was Ben. He immediately took the cover off my eyes, and loosened the rope so I could sit up. I had tears rolling down my face and Ben reached over to the table by the window and poured me a glass of water. I drank down the water in one gulp and held out the glass.

"I'm sorry this happened to you. I won't let it happen again."

"That is Frank Wallberg!" I blurted it out and waited for his response.

"Yes, it is Frank."

"How do you know him?"

"It's a long story, and I really don't think it is necessary to get into it right now."

"You are not like him, and I don't understand why you are with him."

"Let's just say that one day, a long time ago, Frank helped me out when I needed it, and now it's my turn to return the favor."

I wasn't happy with his answer, but for now, all I could think of was breathing and slowing down my heart rate.

"I won't leave you alone again with Frank, I promise."

It totally confused me. If he cared what happened to me, then why did he take me in the first place? This made no sense at all.

"Ben, I want to know what is going on here. I think you owe it to me to explain this. Why did you take me, and why am I tied up here?"

"Like I said it's a long story, and I don't want to get into it."

"Well, it looks to me like we have all kind of time, so tell me what is going on. Why is Frank so bitter? And why are you involved with him?"

chapter 16

Gunn entered Ruby's house from the front. There was no time to walk around behind the house and see if anyone was around. If there was someone in the house, he would catch them red handed. He kicked open the door, and there was no one around. He walked from room to room with his gun drawn. The house was empty.

Gunn went into the basement to look for clues. Maybe there was something in those boxes that would help him figure out what Ruby's involvement was with Wallberg. He sifted through piles of papers and came up empty handed. He looked around the room and noticed a box up on the top shelf with loads of dust on it. He walked over and brought the box down. It was filled with more papers and pictures. Gunn looked through the pictures very carefully. Ruby was in a few of the pictures, and there was a very beautiful young women with her. It must have been her daughter. He came across another picture of the same woman holding a baby. He wondered if Ruby's daughter had a child or was it someone else's she was holding. He took some of the pictures and put them in the inside pocket of his jacket. He found some bank statements and grabbed those too. Possibly Ruby's daughter could answer some questions for them. At that point, Ruby's daughter still hadn't shown up in Daywater.

Gunn went up the stairs and looked around one more time. He

decided to go back to the station and see if Max could tell him who the people in the picture were. He got back to the station and walked in on Max going through some paper work. The anguish in Max's face told a story on its own. Max wanted this case solved and closed as soon as possible.

"Max, can you have a look at these pictures and tell me who this is?"

"Sure, bring them over." Max carefully looked at them and immediately spoke up. "That is Ruby's daughter, Trina, and you know, I always wondered about the gossip that was going around here."

"What gossip is that?"

Max shook his head and looked right at Gunn. "Well, the word around here a while back was that Trina and Jack Wallberg had an affair. Apparently, Trina got pregnant, and Ruby shipped her off somewhere. This kind of thing doesn't happen here, and it wouldn't have been accepted very well. There was also talk that Frank was totally in love with Trina but she would never go out with him. I can't imagine why?" Max chuckled and Gunn looked at him puzzled.

"Why are you laughing?"

"Well, Frank was just as crazy then as he is now. No one hung around with him even before he got into trouble. Frank was a loner, a strange bird you might say. But now things might just come together. If Trina was pregnant with Jack Wallberg's baby, and let's just say Frank found out about it, how do you think he would feel about that?"

"I don't imagine he would have been too happy to find out his Dad was doing the love of his life."

"No, I don't think he would be too happy about that. That would probably be enough to push him over the edge and try to take away anything that made his father happy. That's why all the killings."

"Of course, especially after Ruby sent Trina away. That would have really upset him. Then he wouldn't see her at all."

"Has there been any word, Max, on when Trina will be getting here?"

"Not a word, which I think is kind of strange. I mean this is her mother and you would think she would want to be here for the funeral at the very least."

Just then the door opened at the station house and in walked a very beautiful young lady.

"Hello, I'm Trina, and I'm here to find out who killed my mother."

Max quickly stood up and walked over to her. He pulled a chair out from behind a desk and asked her to have a seat.

"I'm sorry about Ruby. She was well liked around here, but I know that you already know that. You have been gone for quite some time now. You haven't changed a bit from what I remember."

Trina blushed and responded in a friendly fashion. "I guess your memory isn't that great then, is it?" We all smiled, and Max spoke up again.

"Trina, we don't have the killer yet, but we are hoping that you can answer some of our questions and it just might help us to find him and possibly piece together why it is that all of these people had to die."

"What do you mean all of these people?"

Trina looked startled, she obviously hadn't heard about the Wallbergs.

"Trina, Jack Wallberg and his wife Sabella have been murdered. So have all of their employees."

The look on Trina's face was total shock, and she quickly stood up and walked towards the window. You could see that she was very upset by the information she had just received. Max walked over to her and put his arm around her shoulder, "Trina come and have a seat. I know this is a lot of bad news for you to get all at once." She walked over with Max and sat down again in the chair. Gunn walked over to the counter and poured a glass of cold water and then handed it to Trina. She took the glass and with tears running down her face, she drank the water. Max pulled up a chair and sat down beside her, "Trina, we have a lot to talk about."

"All of these people died because of me!" Trina was sobbing and holding her head in her hands. "If I hadn't done what I did, everyone would still be alive. My Mom! Of all people, how could this happen?"

Gunn and Max sat there and listened. At times like this it was best to say as little as possible and let the person talk.

"Trina, what are you saying? What did you do that you shouldn't have done?"

"I fell in love with Jack Wallberg. I was young, but he gave me what I needed. He made me feel loved and needed. He bought me things, and he took me places. My mom told me to stop seeing him when she found out about us, but it was too late. I had gotten pregnant. When I told Jack, he wanted nothing more to do with me. I had no choice but to go to Mom and tell her that he turned me away. She told me not to worry, and that she would take care of everything. I had to trust her. I know she went and spoke to Jack several times but didn't get anywhere with him. Then, one day she came back from seeing Jack and gave me an envelope full of money. I don't even know how much was in there. She told me this was for me and the baby and that it was time for me to leave Daywater. She set me up in New York with some family, and I stayed with them until the baby was born. Then, I moved out and got my own place. I have been there ever since. I did call her two weeks ago and told her that I was thinking about moving back because I was running out of money. She told me to stay right there, she would see to it that I get more of what was coming to me and the baby. That was the last I heard from her."

Max and Gunn sat back and looked at each other. Things were really starting to take form. It was coming together now why Ruby was there at the Wallberg's. She was there to get more money for her daughter, and for Jack's child, to live. It was totally understandable that she would go there. It is sad though that she must have gotten in the way of the killer and died instead. But where did Frank fit into all of this? Why is he so squeaky clean right now? Up to this point, he hadn't killed anyone, and in fact, all murders were performed by Benjamin Gale. Could Frank actually be thinking that if he gets rid of everyone around him that he will be the sole inheritor of the estate? Did he think that this would be enough to get Trina to come with him? Anything was possible, Gunn guessed. But there was still something unanswered. Why did Frank or Benjamin take Meg? It was obvious now that they were working together.

chapter 17

"Ben, so tell me, why are you messed up with Frank?"
"Frank and I were in prison together. I don't suppose you have any idea just how bad it can get there? Well, the blacks ruled the pen, and we didn't like it. The one day all hell broke loose, and I almost lost my life. Frank saved me and I owe him for that."

I was puzzled. Why would someone go to such great lengths and risk their life for this?

"Ben, I wouldn't have thought that you could kill all these people though. I mean, you took lives of people you knew nothing about."

Ben looked away and then spoke with a kind of fear in his voice. "Meg, you don't understand. I had to do this for Frank. If I didn't, then I wouldn't be here right now."

I could see that Ben was trapped by Frank and that was the reason for doing what he did.

"Ben, I think you should untie me, and let's go to the station. You know it's just a matter of time before my partner finds us. If you turn yourself in, I can assure you that they will be made aware of the fact you saved me from being raped by Frank, if not killed. I will help you."

"You can't help me, it's too late."

"Then, at least let me go. I don't know why you are hanging on to me. It makes no sense at all. In fact, I don't understand why you are both still here."

"You don't need to understand, our work isn't finished and until it is, then we will stay here. As for letting you go, I don't think so. We need you, just in case."

It was the just in case that scared me. I would be used as a hostage if things didn't go their way. I could see it now. How would I get away from here? How long before their job was finished? When would Gunn find me? It seemed like forever, and I wanted to be found. In a sense, I was lucky that Ben was here to protect me. But wasn't that ironic? Ben is the killer, and he is the one who has abducted me. Yet, I am relieved he is here. This was making no sense at all.

We heard a car pull up, and Ben quickly tightened my ropes and put the blindfold back over my eyes. He walked out of the room, and I could hear him and Frank talking. They spoke quietly, and it was hard for me to hear what was being said. Frank's tone of voice was excitable. He sounded like he was in a hurry to get things out. I could hear Ben trying to calm Frank down. Then there was silence. Ben came into the room and said, "You are coming with me. I'll take the rope off your hands and feet but don't try anything stupid or you won't live to see another day." Ben was very assertive in his tone of voice. I knew that something was happening. Ben untied my feet and hands. He left the blindfold on and helped me to my feet and then he tied my hands behind me. "You are going to have to come with us."

He led me out of the house, and I could smell the fresh air outside. It had seemed like forever since I smelled the air. It had been so dusty and moldy smelling inside that room that, at times, I felt it hard to breathe. I felt the warm sun on my face and felt the cool breeze blowing through my hair. I heard the trunk of a car pop open and that's when I realized I was going inside. He picked me up and curled me into a fetal position, then placed me in the trunk and closed the lid. I liked the trunk even less than the room. They both got inside the car and sped off the property in a hurry. I knew that Gunn had to be getting close and that's why they had to move me out of there. I bounced around inside the trunk banging on the roof and over to the sides. With my hands tied behind my back, I had trouble trying to brace myself for the bumps and turns that they were taking. Where were we going now?

chapter 18

The phone rang at the station house, and Gunn picked it up right away.

"Daywater Sherrif's Office, Gunn here."

You could see by the look on Gunn's face that the Feds had found something. Gunn hung up the phone.

"Max, the Feds are on to something. I'm meeting them about four miles south of here. Apparently there is an old abandoned farm."

Before Gunn could finish what he had to say, Max looked at him and said, "Go! See what they found."

Gunn grabbed the keys to his cruiser off the desk and hurried out the door. He followed the directions given to him and within minutes pulled up into the yard. There were four state trooper cars parked with the emergency lights on. They were searching the house when Gunn arrived. Agent James Moore met him at the door. "Gunn, I think we just missed them. I have the other Detectives looking for something that might be of help. They have your partner, and by the looks of things, she is still alive."

"Which way do you think they have gone?"

"We know they turned right at the entrance. They were in quite a hurry and almost missed the corner. The tire marks are headed east. I sent two of the guys after them to see if they can catch up to them."

"We have got to find them, Moore, before they decide that Meg is a burden to them."

"I know what you mean. Let's get going."

They got into their own vehicles and quickly left the property in pursuit of the killers. There was a lot of area to cover and to try and find out which way they were going would be next to impossible. As Gunn was more familiar with the country, Moore followed behind him. They reached the first intersection, and you could see where again they had taken a very sharp corner. They were driving very erratically, but it was a good thing because it helped us to know which way they were going.

Way up the road they could see a large cloud of dust. Gunn sped up in an effort to reach the cloud of dust, and hopefully get these guys. When Gunn pulled up, the killer's vehicle was on its roof and the Fed's car parked twenty feet from the vehicle. The two agents were on their knees by their vehicle with their guns drawn. Gunn quickly got out of his car and ran over to the Fed's car. Moore stayed back to cover them. One of the Fed's grabbed a megaphone out of the back seat of his car and raised it to his lips.

"Stay in the car. We are approaching the vehicle. Do not make a move."

The Feds began to slowly walk towards the vehicle. You could see an arm hanging out of the passenger side of the vehicle. It looked limp. One of the other Feds circled around to the driver's side of the vehicle and instantly a shot rang out! The Fed was down. The other retreated. Gunn raised his pistol and pointed it right at the vehicle. He couldn't see the driver from this angle. He tried to go in behind the vehicle, but as soon as he went to move, another gun shot whistled through the air. Gunn dropped to the ground, and he kept his head down to avoid any flying bullets.

Another car with spinning tires raced up behind the police vehicles. The car door flung open and out ran Trina.

"Frank! Frank! It's me, Trina! Please stop this!"

She slowly walked towards Frank. Gunn got up off the ground and tried to get Trina to stop, but she walked right by him.

Frank lowered his gun and looked right at her. "Why did you do this to me? You were mine not my dad's."

"Frank I was never yours and you know that. You have to stop this now. Give me your gun, or you will die. Too many people have

THE WALLBERG MURDERS

died already. Please!"

Frank dropped his gun and laid his head on the ground. He was pinned behind the wheel and couldn't get out. Gunn quickly ran over to the vehicle and kicked the gun out of reach. The other officers grabbed the gun and stepped back. Their guns raised and pointed directly at Frank. They were not going to take any chances in case he had another one. Gunn checked the pulse of the passenger and found none. He bent down and looked into the back seat of the vehicle. He couldn't see Meg anywhere. Then he heard a loud thud coming from the rear of the vehicle.

He looked over at Moore and yelled, "Grab a tire iron! Hurry!" Moore ran over to him and Gunn grabbed the tire iron and pried open the trunk. As soon as the trunk sprang open Meg fell to the ground. The relief on Gunn's face was enough to let everyone know that Meg was alive. She was battered, but she was fine. He scooped her up in his arms and carried her to his car. He never looked back.

chapter 19

Gunn drove straight to the station where Max was patiently waiting. He parked the car right out front. He walked around to the passenger side and opened the door. I was about to get out of the car and again he scooped me up into his arms and carried me inside. Max pulled out the big old chair from his office and Gunn sat me down.

"Meg, I'm so happy to see you. How are you doing?"

"Thank you both. I never thought I'd see the inside of this place again."

Gunn looked over at me and smiled. "Meg, we wouldn't give up on you. You are the best thing that's walked into this place in years."

"So tell me. What has gone on here?"

Max stood up and poured Meg a glass of water. "Are you hungry?"

"Yes, I'm starved but really, I want to know why me?"

Gunn excused himself and left the station telling them he'd be right back. Max looking tired sat down beside me and started to tell me what had all happened to create this tragedy.

"Meg, this Wallberg thing goes back years. Apparently Frank Wallberg was in love with Ruby's daughter Trina, but Trina wouldn't have anything to do with him."

"Was that the girl that showed up and basically saved me from anything else that could have happened?"

"So, she did go there! The radio was turned on, and Moore radioed in to let me know where you guys were and what was happening. She must have heard it because she immediately left the station when I was still on the radio. Well, anyway, Trina was in love with Jack Wallberg, and they had an affair. Everything went along smoothly until Trina got pregnant with Jack's baby. Jack wanted nothing to do with that, so basically, he paid her off through Ruby, and Ruby sent her away to have the child. Frank must have found out and that is what turned him around when he went on a killing spree. He wanted to seek revenge on his father and did so by killing people in an attempt to upset Jack. Of course, he was caught and sat in prison, but as soon as he got out, he started up again right where he left off. Only this time, he would make sure that he dissolved any happiness his father may have had. He had no intention of Jack dying because he wanted him to suffer for taking Trina away from him. Or in his mind, he thought that Jack took Trina away from him."

"But why was Ben involved in this?"

Max got up and walked over and poured himself a coffee.

"Well, Ben and Frank bunked together in prison. Frank saved Ben's life while they were in prison, and Ben promised him that he would pay back the favor. Unfortunately, it was to kill the people close to Jack."

"But, what about Ruby and Little Joe?"

"They were just obstacles that got in the way. Ruby was seeing Jack for more money for Trina to live. She was running out of money and was going to move back and live with Ruby. Although Ruby wanted her to come back, she knew it would be bad if Trina and the baby came back to town. You might say, a bit unsettling for Jack. When she went over to see Jack, she must have seen something, and Ben killed her. As for Little Joe, all we can figure out at this point is that he too got in the way. We can't figure out a reason why he would have been there, but he was definitely in the wrong place at the wrong time. There is some speculation that he may have been seeing one of Jack's hired helpers on the sly."

"What is going to happen to Frank now? And Ben?"

"Well I haven't heard back from the Feds yet but I'm sure they will be coming here soon."

Gunn walked in with a tray full of food. "How's this? I thought I would get you a little of everything. I wasn't sure what you wanted."

"Thank you, Gunn, I'll eat anything right now."

Meg picked up a sandwich that was there and devoured it immediately. She took a bite of a shiny, mouth watering, red apple. She picked up a glass of juice and quickly finished that off too.

"Boy, you were hungry."

Gunn and Max both chuckled. Gunn looked over at Max and asked him if he had heard from Moore. At that moment in walked Moore with Frank Wallberg.

"Where can I put him for the time being?"

Max showed him to the back room cells where they locked him behind iron bars.

"Frank, I guess this is going to be your new home for a little while, until you get transferred to one of the finer facilities."

Max was being sarcastic and slammed the door as he walked out. Moore followed closely behind him.

"Agent Moore, I'd like you to meet Meghan King."

Moore walked over and shook Meg's hand. "It's nice to see we got you back in one piece."

"You'll never know how nice it is to be back in one piece! But tell me, where is Ben?"

Gunn looked over at Meg.

"Meg, Ben is dead. He died when the car rolled. Lucky for him."

Meg quickly spoke up, "You know he saved me from Frank. He had left me in that old farm house, and Frank was on the verge of raping me, and Ben came in. He isn't like Frank."

Max jumped into the conversation at that point. "Well, we don't have to worry about him now. Frank will be put away for life and Ben, well, let's just say he paid his dues."

Gunn got up and walked over to Meg. "Meg, I think it's time to go home now. I'll bet you would like to have a good night's sleep."

"Thank you, Gunn. I'd like that." Gunn placed his arm around Meg and walked her out the door.

The day was over. I couldn't help but ask myself, "What would tomorrow bring?"